FREEMAN'

ISBN 9798672228891
© 2020 LEE K FREEMAN

BELIEFNEXUS.WORDPRESS.COM

Come, let me weave for you a web of wisdom, morals, fables, and other sundry, cautionary tales, where every character has their own story within this veritable jackanory.
So please tell me, dear reader, if you are able,

Who is the teller of these tales and fables?

BELIEFNEXUS@GMAIL.COM

PADRE PETE'S PRELUDE.

Sand and dust were kicked up from under heel as he ran towards the little cabin. Closing the door, he hastily changed from rugged, worn clothes into a white, collared shirt and dark trousers. The collar hung, unpinned from the shirt as he peeked through the window to view his pursuant.

The challenge was that the vagrant could stop his opponent drinking the whisky, without touching him or the glass, before finishing the ale. Everyone wondered how such a feat could be accomplished, to drink a tankard of beer before the other gent could sup his shot of whisky. As there was undoubtedly more ale than whisky, the vagrant was allowed a head start. So he did and opened up his mouth and gullet, pouring the ale straight down his throat in one gulp, then placed the tankard over his opponent's shot of whisky. This not only stopped the shot of bourbon from being drunk but also enraged the man, who then made chase for the vagrant, causing him to flee.

Noticing the hullabaloo, the deputy sheriff wandered over to enquire what was going on. After being informed of the hobo's antics, he ran out of the public house and after him.

Suitably attired, the homeless man opened the cabin door before the constable could land the first knock.

"For whom are you looking?"

The deputy came closer, eyeing the man up and down then said, "A man, about so high and with long hair; a sorry face, and looks like a hobo..."

"Can't help you, I'm afraid. There is only I here, not over there, but here. If any other be near, I would tell you, but there is not, no none other than that of my good self."

"But he came in here, they showed me, pointed this way...."

"They? Who are they?"

"Them!"

"Oh, them! So they are the they, those them over there. Uhmmm... Now are you sure that what they say is true? For congruence is fraught with conformity of confused minds that don't know what they see, save in confirming that which is conformed in the mind of many, by the few, who know what they're doing. So who told you what this man looked like?"

"Well, they did."

"What, all of them, or a few?"

"A few."

"A few you say?"

"Yes, I do."

"Now, what did the first person say?"

"That the thief was a wily son of a gun, lanky, thin, crafty and shifty, longish hair and dirty face."

"And the next? What did they say?"

"That he was so high..."

"How high?"

"This high..."

"Uhm, not so tall then, about average height. Uhm... Now how did others, the rest, describe him?"

"Like a tramp, a bum, a hobo."

"And what has this person done? What crime is alleged to this unfortunate soul?"

"Stealing drink from the bar and tobacco to smoke."

"How was this drink stolen?"

"Via some rouse to drink the beer before another could sup his whisky. The hobo downed the beer and covered the whisky shot with his tankard, thus upsetting the customer."

"Uhm, 'tis crafty as you say. Yet, alas, no man has come past this way. There is only I as you can see, no one else here but me. Now, do I look like someone who would vagrance himself about? A man of good standing, like myself? A man of temperance, modesty and let's not deny it, sober health?"

"No, sir, you don't. So I shall leave you in peace; sorry to have bothered you."

"Tis no bother, good sir."

The constable left the property and walked about trying to find the vagrant, but to no avail.

A sigh of relief fell over the hobo's face as he quickly changed back into his own clothes, but convinced himself that he would only borrow the shoes, the jacket and maybe take a lend of the priest's tunic and dog-collar, for who knew when such a thing would be handy? Then quietly, he slipped out of the back door of the cabin, so to evade the townsfolk.

There was no discernible road or track, but the lingering dust seemed to flit about over flattened ruts where rocks had seemingly made way for the many wagon wheels that had impressed a memory or two over the years. Following the informal route, the vagrant journeyed barefoot, carrying the small bundle of clothes he'd borrowed. Well, he had convinced himself that they were only borrowed anyway. His throat was becoming dry and he was fatigued by the heat of the day. Not many journeyed after the midday and in the full heat of the desert sun. Even the animals knew to wake for the evening of the day, yet here he was limping along the historic route, away from the town and towards another. Finally having had enough, he collapsed to the ground, just off to the wayside. Laying here, he took rest. The sand gently washed and roughed his skin as the slight breeze tried to push a long strand of hair over his left eye. In the very distant, was a familiar sound and as it drew closer he started calling for water. The clip-clop became nearer and he sat up. A haze had formed on the sandy flats and one could just make out the blurry image of a horse and its rider bobbing in time to the clip-clop.

"What on earth are you doing out here in the afternoon sun?"

"Waiting."

"For whom?"

"Someone to bring me water."

"Well, that someone would seem to be me then."

The rider dismounted and brought a canteen over to the hobo. Undoing the lid, he took a sip them passed it to him.

"Much obliged. Don't mind if I do."

"Where yer headin' fella?"

"Oh, that way."

"That's west."

"What town lies that way?'

"Dead in 3 days."

"Ah, right. And which way are you heading?"

"That way; northwest."

"What town lies that way then?"

"Arrive in time for supper."

The rider proffered his hand, enabling the vagrant to stand up. The cowboy clambered on to his horse then helped his passenger to climb on board also, then off they wandered with the gentle clip-clop beginning once more. As the sun began its lazy climb down from the height of day, the horizon began to reveal the tops of wooden buildings.

A sign bore the name, Epiphany, and beyond was a modest town with a saloon, barbershop, railway station and several stores. The rider parked the horse by the railings of the livery. A coin was flipped towards the vagrant, who almost didn't catch it. Nodding his head towards his hero, he thanked him.

"I'll pay you back.."

"Well, that'll take a while, I guess, on account of you havin' bare feet and no sense of direction."

"Thank you again."

Epiphany seemed to be waking up to the cool, moonlit evening, with its occupants milling around from store to store and hotel to saloon. Walking over to the saloon, he could smell the scent of stale and fresh beer, sawdust and whisky. The smell of burnt, fresh tobacco grew stronger as the doors opened, fanning the fragrance towards him.

"I don't suppose I could ask for a cheroot, could I?"

"You suppose right!"

"Ah...."

Moving through to the bar, he ordered a beer and cigarillo. Taking his time to light the cheroot, he looked about, casting his eyes over the customers, knowing which ones to engage and those whom he should ignore.

"You're not from 'round these parts are yer?"

"Is it that obvious? What gave it away?"

"The 3 day odour of perspiration, the look of a hobo and the way you hold that cigar."

"Right, I thought it might have been my English accent."

"What's an Englishman doing in these far flung neck o' the woods?"

"Oh, you know, sightseeing, visiting places, travelling the road less travelled."

"Strange..."

"What's so strange?"

"You seem like a stranger in a strange land, aimlessly wandering from town to town."

"How very astute of you!"

"Well, I'd be careful; the local sheriff dislikes your type. He figures on homeless wanderers beggin' and a-loitering with the intent of no intent. You can bet your life that if he sees you, he'll, well, he'll give you a bed for the night in a 6 by 6 cell."

"Right! Well thank you for the advice. I bid you farewell."

No sooner had the vagrant made his excuses, the sheriff walked in, wearing a bowler hat, waistcoat with a bronze, star-crest badge adorning the upper left chest. Taking a pull on his wide cigar, he straightened himself and walked over to the bar, where the barman poured him a measure of whisky with no words spoken. Looking around, he saw the sandy stranger. The vagrant noticed he'd been noticed and started to move, that was until a baton of some description stopped him in his tracks.

"Now what do we have here?"

"We appear to have a well-oiled baton hindering my progress towards the ablutions. If you'd be so kind..."

"Nope. Ain't no mind to be kind to no hobo. This town ain't for the likes of wanderers."

"So why is there's a hotel across the street?"

"That is for travellers, not aimless amblers."

"Ah, well, I am not a wanderer, nor aimless in my ambling, for I rather need the use of the local ablutions."

"What you doin' here, stranger?"

"Well, odd as it may seem in a saloon, I'm having a drink and cheroot, before bedding down for the night. And I'm rather in need of some urinary relief."

"I mean, what are you doing here in Epiphany? What's your business?"

"I'm a pest control operative, specialising in the controlled removal of Aardvarks."

"Aardvarks? We ain't got no Aardvarks here!"

"I can see my work here is done then...."

"Wait here, my boss will want to speak with you."

The deputy lifted his head slightly and the bowler hat wearing sheriff approached.

"What's your business here, son?"

"I was just explaining to your colleague, that I am a pest controller..."

"He gets rid of Aardvarks," said the deputy.

"We ain't got any Aardvarks!"

"Which means my time here will be very short."

"You're damn right. I have an aversion to Aardvarks and Hobos; both don't linger around these parts, due to my patience, or lack of, for both. Where you stayin' tonight, son?"

"Well, call me crazy, but I was planning using the hotel, for I believe they have an abundance of bedding, beds, hospitality and guests. Now, if you'll excuse me, I really need to use the ablutions...."

"The what?"

"He needs the can!"

"As your colleague says, yes, I need the latrine, the can, the toilet, if you don't mind."

The deputy moved out of the way, letting the vagrant go to the loo. Whilst the vagrant was away, the sheriff looked at the small bundle containing clothes that he had left on the bar, viewing the collar and tunic of a priest within.

"I hope you're suitably relieved. Now, what does an Aardvark loving, pest controller need with the attire of a preacher?"

"It's a hobby really, you know..."

"No, I don't know. Enlighten me..."

"Well if you want enlightenment, you need to speak to a Buddhist monk, not a Christian priest."

"How is being a preacher a hobby? I thought it was a vocation..."

"Er, well, I'm what you may call a part-time preacher, only on Sunday mornings..."

"I see; part-time Aardvark assassin, part-time preacher and full time idiot! What the hell do you think I am? I ain't born yesterday! Get...."

"What a pity! We could have started your personality from scratch!"

"Get him the heck outta here!"

The cell was indeed a 6 by 6 room with solid wooden walls, a small grate was the window in the rear wall and a large metal grid formed the door. Another deputy had locked the vagrant up and was taking his details.

"Name?"

"I don't have one."

"Everyone has a name! Who was you father?"

"Aileen Dover."

"Thought Aileen was a woman's name!"

"He was a very confused man. The name, however, his father carried over, a sort of family tradition..."

"So your father was called Carrie?"

"No, he was Aileen Dover too, or Aileen Dover the second as you Americans say. So, my surname must be, Dover."

"So you're surname is Dover. What's your first name?"

"It might be, Ben..."

"Ben Dover.... What... Enough! Let's call you," said the deputy as he glared at the vagrant, "Smart Alec."

"I don't think I suit, Alec. I don't feel like an Alec. I'm more of a Bartholomew, don't you think?"

"Where you from? How you come to be here?"

"My mother, arguably. Actually, that's a difficult question to answer... Father and mother? My grandparents..."

"Age?"

"No idea."

"What DO you know? Anything?"

"Er, that the total sum of squares on the hypotenuse is equal to the total sum of squares on the opposite two sides..."

"Boy, you better buck up or your neck is gonna swing from the hangman's noose!"

"That might help with this problem I've been having with my back. I feel like I need a good stretch."

"I can assure you you'll get that!"

"Ooo, what time is breakfast? As I can't eat before nine. Upsets my stomach you see."

A long night was endured by the deputy until the dawning sun beckoned the day to begin. Peeking in from the little window within the cell, sun rays warmed and woke the vagrant. The silence was disturbed by the sheriff as he entered the building. An exchange took place between the two lawmen as the hobo rubbed the sleep from his eyes.

"Well, we got you a hearing before the judge this morning."

"On what charge?"

"Vagrancy."

A chunk of bread with cheese and some milk were offered to the prisoner, who took it and ate hungrily. Those few hours between breakfast and court seemed to drag like he was about to be consumed by a black hole, time slowing down the closer he came to the eye of the hole which held his judgement. When the time came, he was chained and taken over to the courthouse, crossing the wide thoroughfare. Yesterday's hero strolled down the street, heading for the livery, tipping his hat in recognition of the not so good morning. Pulling a contorted look on his face, the vagrant attempted to prophecy his impending judgement, being stopped in his muted transaction by yet another deputy who led him.

"All rise for the honourable Justice Makepeace."

The room stood to attention as the judge entered; a man in his late fifties, bald, and wearing spectacles too small for his eyes. After the expected formalities of proceedings, Makepeace addressed the accused.

"You are hereby charged with the crime of vagrancy. How pleads you?"

"Not guilty, m'lud."

"How so?"

"It's all supposition. No one has seen me sleeping rough in this lovely town, nor begging either. In fact I was in the wonderful saloon bar last evening, enjoying a drink and cigarillo, when I was arrested, based merely on my appearance."

"Face it, Mr.... Mr S. Alec, you're not exactly wearing your Sunday best now, are you?"

"Ah, right you are, m'lud. My Sunday best is in my small bundle that I carried with me."

The judge called to see the bundle and opened it slightly to see the crumpled vestment and dog-collar.

"You're telling me you're a preacher?"

"No, you assume that I'm a preacher, just as the law of this town assumed I am a person of no status and without home."

"So what in the Sam Hill are you?"

"I'm a Priest."

"You just said that you aren't a preacher!"

"No, you said I'm a preacher, I said I'm a Priest."

"What's the difference?"

"A preacher, preaches, but a Priest preaches and enables all to partake in the sacraments and can deliver the sacred unction."

"Is this what you were talking about?"

The judge looked to the deputy who had watched over the prisoner the previous night.

"Yes, your honour."

"Hmm... Now if you are a Priest, where's your church? Where's your parish?"

"Well," said the vagrant, "I'm between parishes at the moment."

"So there's no proof you're a preacher either?"

"Save only the proof in my bundle, m'lud."

"That ain't no proof, it just proved you're aloof of somewhere that's devoid of its resident idiot. So unless something can point to the contrary, you will be charged and judged on the issue of being a vagrant."

"If I may, your honour," said a familiar voice from the back of the courthouse. The voice stood up from the congregation and took off his hat.

"I know this man and he ain't done nothin' to no one, except be a nuisance. I was travelling when I happened across his perambulation. He may appear, by all intents and purposes to be a fool, but he is a Priest who is travelling in search of work. He ain't homeless, he's searchin' for a new parish."

"And who are you?"

"I'm proof of this man's story, that's who."

"Well, well. Now I have two men without names!"

"My name is, Samuel J Brooks, yer honour."

The judge stopped and tried to focus on the man at the back of the courtroom.

"Samuel J Brooks? The bounty hunter, Sam Brooks?"

"One and the same."

"My, my! Good to see you, Sam. I take it there's no bounty on this man's head then?"

"If there was, I'd have cashed in on it by now and he would have been in custody. However, it turns out he's in custody and I'm none the richer for it."

"Therefore, I see no crime; Mr whatever your name is, you are hereby dismissed of any charge and free to leave. Case dismissed!"

"That should be the Reverend whatever my name is, but I won't split hairs," said the unaccused, as a sigh of relief came over the vagrant. Being unchained he rubbed his wrists and looked for the bounty hunter, who was making his way out of the court.

"I say, I say, thanks again! I'm indebted to you Mr Brooks."

"You're comin' with me! Bein' as y'all indebted to me 'n all. And zip it. Your problem is that you speak thusly too damn much, at the wrong time, without a hesitation between your mind and tongue, which there should be."

"Where are we going?"

"You'll see."

Sam mounted his horse, stowed his rifle and canteen then offered his hand to the vagrant priest, lifting him up on to the horse. Then off they went through Epiphany and out in to the countryside. Following the train and track for a while, they travelled northwest until the train bent round to the right, at which point they turned left and into sandy desert with peculiar rock formations and remnants of mountains.

"I'm sorry to have caused you any bother and I really do appreciate all your help."

"Uhuh."

"If, I can, in anyway repay you, then I shall."

"There ain't but one way you can repay me. Now mute that hole, before my foot beats yours into that big void you call a mouth."

"Right, okay. I will."

And with that the journey continued in silence. That was until something disturbed Sam. He started to slow the horses pace and adjusted the position of his holster as if getting ready. Hushing the horse, he brought it to a halt then dismounted. Slowly, he moved towards the edge of a cliff and peered over, then went back to the horse and removed the rifle. He beckoned the vagrant to his side and then lay down on the ground and crawled on his belly to almost the very edge of the cliff that overlooked a small valley with a canyon. Using his head to motion the vagrant to see what he saw, he did so. The hobo hadn't been this close to the bounty hunter until now and he noticed the hard worn skin and stubble of the forty-something cowboy, his large hands fitting well worn, leather gloves, the dark brown flecks in his light brown hair, the manly smell and rugged looks of a man who knew what he was doing. Gently whispering to the vagrant, he said, "I want you to go down there and walk in to the canyon."

"I'm to go down there and walk in, right. Then what?"

"Do what you do best, talk."

"And say what exactly?"

"Any damn thing you want! When I give the signal, take cover in those rocks beside the horses."

"What do I say? What if they shoot me? What if they don't engage in conversation?"

"They'll talk when they see you, believe me. And when I give the signal..."

"Take cover behind the rocks beside the horses. Er, what will the signal be?"

"You'll know, trust me."

"Have you thought of, maybe, engaging them in conversation?"

"Nope. These aren't the type of people you talk with; they let their guns do the talkin'. Now get down there."

So the vagrant began his descent into the valley then entered the canyon. Tentatively and carefully, he walked into the canyon.

"Hello. Hello? Hello!! Can I interest you in a new newspaper that's coming out called, Rustler; no, it's not that sort of paper, it's all about rustling and the perils that one can endure as a result of rustling. Yes, it's a niche market, but we feel we've really found our demographic and believe there is room on the market for a newspaper dedicated to the rustling community in this, er, desert."

"Who the hell are you?"

A voice echoed in the canyon aiming towards him.

"Ah, there is someone there, thought there was..."

"Get outta here!"

"Hi, how are you all? I'm a bounty hunter so, if you'd like to come out from hiding, please, and form an orderly queue..."

"Who the hell are you? "

"Like I said, I'm a bounty hunter, sorry if I confused you. If you'd like to form an orderly line... '

"We ain't coming out! You'll just have to shoot us to take us in for the reward."

"Well, I'm a kind of progressive bounty hunter, I find it works best if we all just co-operate and try to get along...."

"There ain't co-operating."

"That's fine. No one likes being a bounty do they? So in situations like these, I do find that negotiating doesn't work, but co-operation does. Now let's start by forming a nice orderly queue and get this over and done with. So who wants to be first?"

"No one wants to be caught, but you move along now and we'll say no more about it; you'll live, we'll live & everyone's happy."

"Now, that's not the co-operation I'm talking about. The type of co-operation I'm thinking of is that you walk out here, arms in the air like the good chaps you are, we take a trip to the nearest marshal, or sheriff, and I collect the bounty, then you go to jail. So let's form a straight line out here now please..."

"We ain't coming out!"

"Now that's not playing by the rules is it? Let's start with something else shall we? How about we get to know each other first. I'm Justin, my favourite colour is pink, I'm a Virgo and like quiet nights in and drinking brandy and soda by a warm log fire. Who's next?"

"What the heck?"

"Come on guys, I've made a start, so who's next?"

"Oh... I'm, I'm Doc, my favourite colour is red, I'm a Sagittarius and I like er, I like, playin' the mouth organ."

"That's great, come on out then, Doc. I really feel we're all starting to bond now and really making progress. "

Doc began to walk out into the open space beyond the horses. Then a thud was heard before a loud bang from a gunshot echoed through the canyon and Doc lay on the ground.

"What the hell was that?"

"That was m'colleague, who's a tad overzealous, but never mind... What's a gunshot between foes, eh? Who's next?"

"You'll just shoot me!"

'No, I won't and I will signal m'colleague to ease up on the trigger, unless you're a Gemini. Ha ha, only joking. Okay. So you, in cave number 1, what's your name? "

"Dennis. And I'm capricious..."

'Well that's brave of you to admit it, but I do feel you maybe meant Capricorn, Dennis. What's your favourite colour? "

"Buh, blue...?"

"Ooo, nice. And what's your favourite drink?"

"Bourbon. "

"Great. So, come on Dennis, come on out and let's see your face."

The cowboy walked out looking about him, showing a well-worn face.

"My, my there's a face only a mother could love. Come over here then, Dennis. If you'd just put these shackles on and stand over there... there we go! And who's left then?"

"His name's Brick. "

"Is that what he is or is it his name? "

"His name's Brick."

"Right, come on then Brick. If you'd like to come out and join the line, please."

Brick walked out into the clear space by the horses.

Another thud was heard as he fell to the floor, then the crack of the gunshot resounded in the canyon.

"Ah, he must have been a Gemini!"

"Why ain't I shot then? "

'You must be worth more alive than dead, Dennis. Anyway, it's been really amazing to meet you. Hope one day we can look back on this, have a laugh and share amusing anecdotes."

Sam began to clamber down into the canyon, listening to the vagrant waffle on to the prisoner. Getting closer, he drew his pistol and when close enough and on level ground, shot Dennis.

"What did you shoot him for?"

"I only had two bullets left in my rifle, but plenty in this pistol, so took out those most likely to argue with their weapons first. This one, he ain't as dangerous, he only shot two people before, but all of 'em can be dead or alive and I prefer the latter. "

"Then what was the point in me endangering my life?"

"Well, the ends justified the means, didn't it and I'll be able to collect the bounty on all of 'em."

"So we're going to cart all three dead bodies to a sheriff?"

"Nope. There's a wonderful new invention, a camera, with which I can line up all three, take a picture of 'em with bullets in their heads, get it developed then provide the proof to the sheriff. And you get your own horse too. Take yer pick from them o'er there and then loose the others."

"Do I get a share of the bounty when you present the picture."

"You got a horse! What more d'yer want?"

"Well I was kind of instrumental in capturing them, so was wondering if I get some of the bounty!"

Sam stopped and thought about it.

"How many did yer kill?"

"None, but I lured them out! Even a fish gets to eat the worm as it's caught. 'Do not muzzle an ox while it is treading out the grain...'"

The cowboy shut up and glared at the vagrant.

"Just get these bodies lined up so I can take their picture!"

Between the efforts of both of them, they managed to line up the men so a photograph could be taken. The hobo even asked the deceased to 'say, cheese,' which gathered another glare from the bounty hunter. When they were done, the large brown camera was stowed on the horse and the two of them rode off.

"Where are you taking me anyway?"

"I know of a town that could do with some divine guidance and as it happens, they have no preacher, so I is taking you there."

"I'm not really a preacher, y'know. I borrowed the clothes... Well, stole them really, as I made away from a drinking game that went sour."

"You're a preacher, trust me."

"I've not had the training and never preached in my life. So I'm not a preacher."

The bounty hunter looked him up and down, gave a half twitch in his left eye, then said, "You're mouthy, loud, contrary and draw attention; in my book that makes you over-qualified!

"I see you more as a, as a Padre. What's your name?"

"Ah, I'm a bit shy when it comes to my name."

"No kiddin,' Mr S Alec?!?"

The horses began entering a rocky valley with peculiar shaped rocks had been shaped by the ancient rivers of yore. In the cliffs, varying layers of strata told of tides and events from thousands of years ago. The horses found some of the rock slopes awkward to navigate but managed to bring their riders safely through.

"Besides, I'm a miserable sinner. I've lied, cheated, stolen and been a terrible human being, so how can I be a preacher?"

"Like I said, you're over-qualified. You're not saving yourself, you'll be saving others. It ain't about the messenger, it's about the message. Ain't no one perfect in this world."

"So you're saying, 'let he who is without sin cast the first stone?"

"Yep."

The words had no sooner left his mouth, when a precipice let its grasp loose a large rock to fall inches away from the vagrant. The cowboy had a silent, single chuckle and said, "I think someone's tryin' to tell you somethin'!"

The hobo looked upwards.

"I rather think that you're right. I never thought a second chance, so to speak, would come through a bounty hunter."

"Look, I don't know who or what you are, but what I do know is that you're a well-spoken, wandering, English dude and someone, somewhere will be looking for you. All I do know is that you're allegedly a preacher, so preach. I'm giving you a chance, son, so take it; show 'em the error of their ways. And if I ever happen to be lookin' for a skinny, white Englishman with an attitude and price on his head, well I may just frequent this place we're travellin' to and see if it's worthwhile cashing in on that. You got me? Good. So be a preacher and preach."

The would-be preacher bowed his head, thought about what the bounty hunter said.

"V.."

"Don't tell me. Don't tell me your name, otherwise I'll have to remember to forget I ever heard of yer. Just think of a name for your ordination, Padre."

As they journeyed, names and ideas were exchanged. After a short while, the horizon revealed a small town with a modest steeple ringing out a peel to the impending sunset. Getting closer, the duo pressed onwards.

"Padre Peter?."

"Pete."

"That'll do. Padre Pete , it is."

Riding into the town, they passed by the rotten, wooden sign bearing the town's name, Pity. A few townsfolk lingered about the main street, staring at the two horsemen. Sam dismounted first and beckoned Padre Pete to do the same, then tied the horses to the nearby rail.

"Fetch out, Dorothea will yer!"

"They'll never believe I'm a preacher!"

"There's always a lie in believe. Don't you realize that no matter what anyone believes, there's still always a lie involved - don't matter if you say or spell it."

A chubby woman came over, wearing a well-worn apron over a gingham dress with petticoats trying to escape from under the skirt.

"Well, as I live and breathe, it's Sam Brooks! My goodness, how good to see you!"

"Dorothea, I'm a man of my word and have found you a preacher. In fact, better than that, what we have here is a Padre."

Padre Pete extended his grubby hand to shake Dorothea's.

"So nice to meet you."

"This sure doesn't look like a Padre."

"Wait til he's all washed up. Both he and I have days of travel needin' to be washed off," said Sam as he wiped some desert dust off of his clothes. Dorothea looked Pete up and down.

"Where's his collar?"

"He ain't a dog, Dorothea!"

"All preachers have a collar. Where's his?"

Pete patted his small bundle. Looking around, he spied a saloon, stores, Barber shop, post office and railway track with a small, single coach sized station. A few houses were visible and they extended beyond the main road going through Pity. At the far side of the town was a small, modest church with a bell hanging in a small tower on top of the roof. Dorothea beckoned the Padre to follow her and led him to her home. After boiling copious amounts of water and filling an old trough, Pete stepped in to bathe. The warm water soothed his skin as another bucket of cold water was poured in the make-do bath.

After an hour or so, a clean and shaven Padre emerged from the bathroom wearing his black shirt and white collar. Looking more like a respectable man of the cloth should now, he sat down to eat with his host.

"Well now! You're certainly looking the part!"

"Thank you for the use of your bathroom. I feel more human now."

"Tell me, where you from?"

"England."

"And what brings you over here?"

"Life."

"I see. Such a queer river is life, isn't it?"

The two of them chatted as they ate, then after the meal, she took him on a tour of the church, which comprised of a small hall, a tiny office and a lectern on a podium which elevated him two feet above the congregation.

"How many attend?"

"Oh, not many these days. A lot have stopped coming since Father Stephen got shot..."

"Got shot?"

"Yes, after his sermon on turning the other cheek. There's just a few now, maybe a handful, or possibly three..."

"Three handfuls?"

"No, just three. We do have a piano player though, Miss April."

Pete looked at the hall and took his place at the lectern. Looking out towards the back of the hall, he imagined what it would be like to preach here.

"Well, you must be wanting to rest, as you've had a long journey and have a sermon to prepare an' all. Where exactly did you study and get ordained?"

"The, er, the Saint, Saint Rupert, er, Ecclesiastical College of hmm, er, of Minsk."

"The Saint Rupert Ecclesiastical College of Minsk? Where on earth is that?"

"Belarus, I think..."

"So let me get this right; you're an Englishman with a Spanish title from a Slavic-Russian college, who's now livin' in America."

"Yes, that's correct."

"Get around quite a bit don't yer!"

"That I do, dear lady. And now I'm here with you in this wonderful little town."

"Well, I'm sure you'll fit in just fine."

And he thought he would too, as long as he could write a sermon, which he had never done before. The mere thought made him panic, which must have led to him accidentally tripping over and hitting his head on the floor. As he fell, he had tried to steady himself on the lectern, which fell with him and landed on top of his head.

"Padre? Padre?"

There was no response. Pete tried to open his eyes, but was met only by a large cat licking his eyelids and purring rather loudly. Amidst his struggles to get up, the pampering puss-cat, the lectern heavily leaning on his chest and Dorothea fretting, the church began to spin around, so much so that his head fell back on the wooden floor, rendering him unconscious.

Introducing Marmalade.

"Behold, I have arrived, oh chosen one," announced a strange, unfamiliar voice, which then muttered under its breath, "What a stupid place to put the water!"

The catflap clattered and a kerfuffle was heard at the back door. An anxious kitten awoke and tried to see what was happening, but was unable to discern the cause of disruption.

"So much for a grand entrance! The Superior Cosmic Being gets resplendent, bright lights, choirs of messengers singing its arrival, but me, no, what do I get? A catflap that's too small, a soggy foot, utter darkness and a racket loud enough to wake the dead! For heaven's sake, it's not much to ask is it, really?!"

"What's gannin' on? I cannit see! I cannit see," cried a young cat, from somewhere in the kitchen.

"Hang on!!! Open your eyes… Chuffin' catflap," said the irritated voice.

"My eyes are open, but I cannit see!"

"It's ok, dude, just chill yer beans," said the unannounced visitor. "One of the humans probably hasn't turned the light on yet."

"But it's so dark and I cannit see anything."

A loud bump was heard.

"Well maybe just chill out dude, sit down and don't move about until your eyes adjust, or you'll bump into something."

"Too late, just done that!"

"One of the beings will turn the light on soon! Just sit still, chill, relax and... Somebody turn the freakin' light on!"

As the hullabaloo settled, darkness encompassed the young cat and its visitor. The usual noises could be heard, seeming so unusual in the darkness, making the kitten twitchy and jumpy.

"What was that?"

"What now? What was what?"

"That... There it is again!"

"What?"

"That noise..."

"What noise?"

"That tappin' noise."

"The tapping noise?"

"Yes, the tappin' noise! What is it?"

"It's the bloomin' tap. For pity's sake! Chill yer beans, dude. Just relax. For a 'chosen one' you're rather anxious. I was expecting some bold, fearless tiger!"

The dripping water on the metal sink echoed through the still property. As their eyes adjusted to the dark light, the guest cat lay down next to whimpering kitten and closed his eyes.

"How can you go to sleep at a time like this?"

"Any time is a good time to sleep and I definitely need a nap after such a failed entrance," said what appeared to be possibly another cat, as it flexed its long tail before slouching to the floor alongside him.

"What about the perils within the darkness? What if somethin' breaks in and eats us? What if a zombie dog should wander in and take us in its mouth, that stinks of rotten flesh? What if…"

"…you shut up & stop worrying? Chill, relax, let those beans cool down."

Yawning, the visiting moggy settled down once more, as the timid, dark, tabby lay beside him shivering nervously. Every little sound made the young cat jump and gasp. His wide, dark eyes searched the dim room which they were in, looking for would-be monsters that lurked under chairs, units & tables.

"I don't think I can put up with this much longer, man."

"Okay, okay. Let's try this again, sans catflap and water… Lo, I am here, oh chosen one! I come to reveal and explain to you the secrets of the mystical arts!"

"What mystical arts?"

"Thee mystical arts, which work with us and through us since the dawn of time until the end of everything, when the universe dissolves and everything becomes a custard like substance, without vanilla extract for favouring. I have approached you to teach you the principles of these mysteries that work, in, through and with us. Sound good to you? "

"Er, okay."

"Good. Now, then, first things first, what is your name?"

"Er, Puddles."

"Nice to meet you, Er Puddles. A curious name indeed, for a 'chosen one.' Why are you called, Puddles? Enlighten me."

"Whenever I get scared, I pee me-self, yer see."

"Hmm. That probably explains the ad hoc placement of water within this kitchen. I fear I may have stepped in some earlier... Anyway, young Er Puddles, my name is, Marmalade and..."

He paused, looking at the small kitten and examining him. An almost surprised look grew on his face as he pulled back and reviewed the small, nervous Puddles.

"So you're the 'chosen one'?"

"Am I?"

"Yes apparently so..."

"What's a 'chosen one'?"

"A hero, a messenger, a bringer of hope! I never expected it to be a small, incontinent, timid tabby. Anyway, who am I to judge? So, young Puddles, I have been sent to teach you the mystical arts. So, first of all, we're going to turn that bloomin' light on by staring at that white panel on the wall."

"Starin' at the panel? Doesn't seem very mystical, mind."

"Yes, by staring at that white panel on the wall. Eventually the light comes on, trust me."

So they stared at the small, white rectangle on the wall which encased the light switch. Marmalade began making a purring sort of noise as he contemplated. The staring continued for a good while, in silence.

"I'm bored," said Puddles.

"Keep going bro', keep going. Just relax into it. This is called contemplation, dude, and it's part of the mystic arts, alongside meditation, the law of attraction and how not to get yer butt kicked by Mildred, who lives at 52 Blythe Crescent. So just focus your attention on the white panel."

The two cats continued to stare blankly at the small white panel on the wall beside the door and after a short while, the door opened slowly. Puddles gasped. As the door hinge creaked, a feint trickle of water could be heard, then a hand began to reach in, moving across the wall and eventually turned the light on.

"Bingo!" yelled Marmalade.

The sudden exclamation made Puddles jump, yet he also looked amazed. "Wow! How'd yer dee that?"

"The mystical arts, dude, the mystical arts..."

However, after considering what happened, Puddles gained a curious look on his face.

"Hang on... Are you sure it was the mystic arts? It seemed like one of the humans came in and turned the light on!"

A frown adorned Marmalade's face, so he got up and paced around the kitten, in a rather disappointed mood, giving the kitten a chance to observe his tutor and notice the long-haired, ginger, Persian cat's physique, his size, poise and posture. Placing his visage right in front of the kitten's face he narrowed his eyes.

"I don't like the cynicism, dude. If you are to learn the ancient secrets from me, you need to open your mind and be less judgemental! I can't deal with negative energy, okay dude?"

Pulling himself back from the kitten he continued.

"So, you're probably wondering what teachers of the mystical arts do; well, we reveal things, prophesy things, ponder things, know things, tweak things, deliver messages about things, have visions regarding things... Oh, and write lots of poetry."

"That's, that's lots of things."

"And poetry, don't forget the poetry, dude."

"What's poetry?"

Marmalade cleared his throat and poised himself to perform a poem.

"When the Supreme Being requireth a task,

Like delivering a message, or a 'Get Well' card,

Do as we must, for the great Being, to whom we pray,

Such things as the shopping, or cleaning the litter tray.

No job is too little or too large,

Whether 'tis to fetch forth heroes, treats, or a packet of lard."

There was a pause, a silence for what potentially would be applause, but none came. Marmalade looked at Puddles, who had a blank expression covering his face, then sighed.

"Right then, lesson numero one, interconnectedness. All things are inexplicably entwined. For example, the light gives life to the corn, the corn makes cereal, in which milk is poured, which is consumed by catlets and other beings. Thus, all things are connected."

Puddles looked perplexed. "How?"

"Listen again: the light gives life to the corn, the corn makes cereal, on which milk is poured, which is then consumed. So the cow and corn become entwined. Nature doesn't make an animal that produces both cereal and milk, does it? No! In fact what would that creature even look like? Part cow, part plant? Part animal, part cereal? What would it be called? A kellogcow? A nestlegoat? And what would it produce?

Shredded cowturd? Maltedmilkicles? Anyway... I digress. All things are interconnected, dude, all things."

"I see!"

"Do you? Do you?"

Puddles continued to sit as the preaching puss walked around and around in a virtual circle created to keep the student in the centre, but this was making Puddles giddy, as his head tried to keep up with following Marmalade on each circuit.

"Stop! You're making me dizzy!"

"Let me ask you, how did everything come about? How was everything created? Do you know? Do you know? No!"

A silence followed and Marmalade kept nodding in a motion to encourage the kitten to say something, anything, or ask a question. Each time he nodded, his eyebrows went higher, his wide eyes encouraging some response from Puddles.

"Sorry... So, how was everything created?"

"I'm so glad you asked; cans."

"What?"

"Everything comes from cans."

"Everything?"

"Everything. And for the cans, there's hands."

"Hands?"

"Yes, hands for the cans in the vast expanse."

"Hands for the cans in the vast expanse?"

"YES! Yes, hands for the cans in the vast expanse. And verily, I say unto you, the Superior Cosmic Being is the one with the hands that holds the cans that fill the expanse. For when anything is created, it comes forth from one of these cans, pre-packaged by the shops in big trays, which apparently are on offer (and it's cheaper to bulk buy, sayeth the beings who feed us) within the great cathedral they call Tescobury's."

"What's Tescoburys?"

"It's the place the beings go to get stuff, just as the Superior Cosmic Being does. This is a mysterious place that all things are brought forth from; cream, marshmallows, underwear, hamburgers, doilies, pot pouri, umbrellas, mangos, light aircraft... Anyway, they go there, are away for what seems like an eternity, then return with lots of cans and things they let go rotten before throwing out - some kind of ritual I think...

"In short, us catlets have a can-centric philosophy whereby everything revolves around cans. This differs from human beliefs, which are very hard to keep up on, as, parenthetically, there's so many of the bloomin' things! Anyway, our can-centric philosophy is a neo-post-Napoleonic idea propagated by the cats of the Frankish empire which succeeded the tertiary ideas of the proto-Egyptian ideology. It's an idea, not a belief system, as opposed to the doglings who appear to venerate the beings that cater to their every whim. Bowing before them, doing cute tricks, et cetera. 'Oh, who's a clever boy?!' Clever my eye! Dogs are slaves and once they're emancipated goodness knows what will happen! Anyway, moving on...

"Our can-centric ideas mean we believe that, arguably, everything comes from cans, as well as the notion that we CAN do anything with the will of the Superior Cosmic Being, who empowers us by sharing, what ports to be, a supernatural force which enables all things to live in the multiverse."

Puddles looked amazed yet confused, trying to make sense of what he was being told.

"What's a multiverse?"

"Well, there's a universe is in each of us, just as we are in this universe and we each also exist in the minds of those whom we visit and meet. So you exist as you, alongside the versions of you, that are in the minds of those you encounter. In each of these minds, another version of you exists, hence this multiverse scenario."

"I see."

"Anyway, attention please; in the beginning there was the Superior Cosmic Being who opened a can & everything came out, and light was also poured out so the cosmic being could see to do the stuff it needed to do, as it couldn't see what it was doing, you see. Then this same cosmic being built a house in some space, then built furniture to fill the space, even though there was still a lot of space not filled all over the place. After this, the being created more lights; the silver night light, the gold day light and the internal lights, which the humans seem to leave on even when it's light, although they don't need it on... Anyway, after the furniture and stuff, animals just started appearing, being brought home by the beings after they said, 'Ah, isn't it sweet, shall we get one? Can we? Can we?' Thus, dudes, dudettes, catlets & doglings, birdies, lizards, snakes and phones were created. In fact, pretty much anything the humans speak to was brought home, really."

"Phones?"

"Yeah, phones. They are a wierd, electronic pet that the humans constantly communicate with. They shout, talk and bicker with them and spend endless hours making stupid poses so take selfies, whatever they chuffin' are... Anyway, after this the Superior Cosmic Being (or SCB as I call it) looked about, liked what it saw, then sat down and chilled out a bit."

"Wow! So, is the supreme cosmic bean immortal?"

"It's beyond comprehension, both created and uncreated, a bit like those black bits you find in fur-balls; how do they get there! I don't know! Is it lint? What is it? What is it? It is indeed most curious. Anyway, unlike us catlets, the SCB is eternal, all powerful, all knowing and seems to be everywhere at the same time. Bit like the twins, Bubbles & Milky, at 9 Heathside Gardens. The SCB is beyond time, but in time, on time and ahead of its time, a bit like the dude, Christopher Nolan."

"So this supreme cosmic bean is older than anyone?"

"Superior Cosmic Being! Not bean! Mind you beans do come from cans don't they... You might have something there... Anyway, it has more than the nine lives we have, for it is immortal!"

"How many lives do we have?"

"Well, they say a catlet has nine lives; each life is measured by 823 cans, except for a leap life, which has 824 cans, and occurs every 4th life. However, some catlets have lived for 12 lives and there's rumours that Ermintrude at 14, Osmotherly Drive is actually 15 lives old! I think she's possibly older though; she's mad as a hatter, losing her marbles and keeps singing, 'Happy Birthday' to the cockatiel at 32 Dewsbury Gardens. 'Happy birthday to you, happy birthday to you! Happy birthday dear Buttercup... Happy birthday to you!' Anyway..."

Puddles' jaw dropped at the knowledge and wisdom of Marmalade, looking totally amazed and in awe of the mystic moggy.

"How de yer nah all this stuff, like?" quizzed Puddles.

"I learnt from the gurus, studied the greats, received transmissions of wisdom from the master dudes and had catnip with Ghandi, who was a pretty cool dude - well his cat was anyway; some long-haired bit from Darussalam who had a compulsion to have lavender water in jasmine tea. Which is absolutely disgusting, I can tell you..."

"You knew Ghandi's cat?"

"Yeah, I did. I'm as old as the hills, dude. Anyway, come with me and I'll show you some more of the mystical arts."

The two cats left the comfort of the kitchen and went upstairs to the bathroom and sat on the toilet.

"Why are we in the bathroom?" asked Puddles, looking at the shower curtain, wondering if he could climb it like the other curtains in the house.

"This is the wisdom seat."

"This is the human's toilet."

"Dude, it's the Wisdom seat."

"No, it's a toilet."

"Wisdom seat."

"Toilet."

"Wisdom seat!"

"Toilet!"

"Wisdom seat!! Believe me, this is the wisdom seat, for humans use it to do their deepest thinking, as well as pass through poo and wee. I have seen them, sitting on here, with much concentration on their faces, deliberating over issues whilst defecating. And believe me, it works for us catlets also. It is rumoured that Abdul the Mongolian catlet dude ruminated on a human toilet seat lid for many hours when he received the great prophecy..."

"Prophecy? What's a prophecy?"

"Don't you know anything about your rich, cat heritage?"

"Er, not really, nah! Oh, I do remember me dad tellin' me about the Great Catman. He'd say, 'There's that Great Catman!' I was very young at the time..."

Marmalade had a look of bewilderment about him, saying, "I've never heard of a 'Great Catman,' before...."

Then Marmalade thought about it further.

"Where are you from, young Puddles?"

"From 'round Sunderland way, think I was born in Ryhope..."

"Wry-hope? Sounds like a scornful whim on a fanciful day, doesn't it...? Right, and tell me, did you frequently see a grey cat at all?"

"Aye, I did that! Yer right!"

"Hmm; I do fear that you have not picked up on the subtleties of your own Mackem accent and its associated vernacular. So I deduce that there's no 'Great Catman,' but a grey cat, man."

"Ah, reet. You could be right there mind."

"Yes, I'm pretty sure on this as I have read through vast tomes of literature and have never heard of a, 'Great Catman!'"

Marmalade rolled his eyes, almost in despair, then proceeded to lecture the kitten.

"Anyway, prophecy. Now, prophecy is a great, encouraging message regarding the future, of what is, what was and what isn't yet to come; a bit like the sequel to Titanic. If you haven't watched it, you must; crackin' film with Billy Zane in. You don't see much of Billy Zane these days, do you...

"Anyway, Abdul the Mongolian, he had this message from the toilet lid of Genghis Khan: And it shall come to pass that there shall be signs in later times that the great cat awakening shall occur henceforth, therein, hitherto, sometime or other, in the near future or late future, sometime soon, possibly, maybe even tomorrow. Yet they won't recognise the signs, although some might, but not all, just a few, maybe a handful, possibly more. And the few who recognise these things that come to pass will be of the elect few who have been chosen ahead of time, ordained in the past, that has not yet happened, but will assuredly occur, but not yet, sometime therein, hitherto, henceforth in the days of future's past. And these shall be the signs which the elect will observe; there shall be a shift towards the cat litter becoming eco-friendly and made of tree bark. Cans will be sold in multipacks, each bearing the warning, 'Not to be sold separately,' and fish sticks will be renamed fish flavoured sticks, due to a trades description foul-up as there is no fish in fish sticks apparently, merely a flavouring reminiscent of crabs, white bait and herring. Then there shall be other signs; the toilet roll will empty, the air freshener will run out, and when one wants the loo, it shall not be vacant.

"But these are only the beginnings for, lo, a great man cometh having the name Simon, who doth wear a cowl and he shall tell us what we shall listen to, by way of music and songs shall be released, cover versions that have a key change after the last verse of the song.

"Pay heed to these signs, for 'tis when they come to pass that you will know that there will be a great awakening for us cats. Then things will disappear a bit, but reappear in other places and they will say, 'But I never left it here!' But their partners will say, 'Yes you did leave it there, you just don't remember, as you're very forgetful these days' 'No, I definitely didn't leave it there!' 'Yes, you did; you're always doing this?' 'What?' 'Saying you never left it there when you actually did!' 'Oh, don't start this again...'

"AND more things will happen. Lost socks will emerge to be united with the socks they left behind, things that had been hidden will be unhidden, things that went east will go west, things that went north will go south, things that went right will go left, things that went left shall go right, things that went up..."

"Will gan down?" said Puddles .

"Oh, you know the great prophecy then do you?"

"Nah, was just a guess."

A stern look of questioning mixed with a half closed, discerning, focused eye, came from Marmalade, giving pause to the oration.

"And lo, there will come a time when the veil will be lifted and all things will be revealed; in the truth, we shall discover what makes and binds all things together, what's really under the cushion covers, what occasions occasional tables are used for, whatever happened to Dire Straits, why the table cloth has that stain on it that won't come out with a stain remover, why things are here and not there, there and not here, why Dickens the cat from 16 Sycamore Avenue has that unusual squeak in his tail; how Dreamytime Cheesy Chews have that tangy something that makes them a real treat, how Michael Bublé is so brilliant. And we will know the answers to questions of existence; why are we here, what is our purpose, what is the meaning of being, the meaning of life, and why do humans only put the bins out for Tuesday mornings? Yes, all these will be answered and more, when the time cometh and the moon languisheth in the east, when the sun sets in the west. When thou hast seen these signs, there shall be the unveiling of all things and you shall know the truth and understand all things."

"Wow."

"Yeah and y'know what? The dude kinda got it right. Why is there no sequel to Titanic? Why is Michael Bublé so brilliant? And why is it we only see him at Christmas? Does he hibernate in Canada for the rest of the year? I don't know, I don't know! Anyway, come hither young Puddles, let us go outside to the back garden."

Off they went, down the stairs, through the kitchen and out of the cat flap to the garden at the rear of the property.

"Pay attention. Next I shall teach you about humans. What have you learnt about them thus far in your short existence?"

"Not much mind; they talk a lot, feed us and clean up the sh*t in the litter tray."

"Poo. It's cat poo, not sh*t. Mind your language... Uhm, so you don't know much then. Well, let us begin with the basics. They like to baby us, talking in silly voices and they enjoy being ironic. They say things like, 'Now you know that you shouldn't be up there don't you?' When we do actually want to be up there! That is why one IS going up there! And they like to think they're in control. A nota bené here; let them think they are in control but keep control by eating your food when you want to and occasionally poop somewhere other than the litter tray, just to keep them on their toes! They are also very precious about their possessions, so if you happen to break say, a vase, they go absolutely nuts and want to kick you.

"These humans also have an infinite number of uses for soaps and detergents which are branded for individual use, but are ultimately all the same thing, just marketed to target areas for ultimate profits. What's really weird though is that the middle class beings like to pay more as they think that paying more seems better, whereas, the poorest & richest like to save money by paying a reasonable amount.

"The humans also like to badge and label themselves so people can see what they are 'into.' They brand themselves and find identity in labels which is most peculiar, as when they reach middle age, they want to 'discover' themselves, by dropping all the labels then putting them all back on in some sort of catharsis.

"Then there's the bedroom, in which they all love to sleep in and often make weird noises in here; groans and shouts can be heard periodically which makes one wonder what they are up to... If you find one human is in bed, nudge up to them with your nose or mouth, purr and miaow and you can get lotsa hugs and strokes. And when they annoy you, pee on their pillow; it satisfies you and makes them buy a new one which are thee best things to sleep on. I love new pillows nearly as much as I love tuna mayonnaise with olives and capers.

"Then there's this bizarre belief in karma. Some believe that if they do bad, bad things will happen back to them and likewise the same for good deeds. Yet they fail to see that it's just life happening. Plus they seem to think they can eat karma, which is a rather delicious, creamy dish with meat and lots of lovely rice.

"They also rise and rest with the sun which arises over there in the east, goes down in the west & the moon comes up after the sun goes to bed and goes wherever it bally wants, I think that's due to some sort of cosmic wobble. So that's the humans, in a nutshell!"

Puddles struggled to take in all that was happening. Marmalade continued to explain the mystical arts to his protégé whilst pacing the garden and occasionally jumping on to a fence or gate. He moved on to explain visions and their impact on cats, how it was a deep movement within the souls of both the cat and the universe which brings them closer to the Supreme Cosmic Being.

"I had a vision once, y'know."

"A vision?"

"Yes, a vision, a visitor came to me. I was in the kitchen once, resting on the cool floor tiles and there, before me, I saw a resplendent light and this presence beckoned me, with a soft, gentle voice, saying, 'Marmaduke, Marmaduke...'" And I said, 'I'm sorry but my name's not Marmaduke, it's Marmalade.' And it replied, 'Sorry, Marmalade, I can't see properly for this light, it blindeth my eyes, it's a bit bright, isn't it?' And I replied, 'Yes, it is. Have you a dimmer switch? Maybe turn it down a notch.' And the voice returneth, saying, 'I'm afraid we don't have a dimmer switch, as it's an imperial fitting and the dimmer switches are all metric I'm afraid.' So I said, 'Why don't you try going to Homebase or another suitable hardware store?' Then the voice replied, 'No, I can't I'm afraid as we lost our trade card; we can only buy wholsesale you see.' And I replied, 'Well, try Wilkinsons, they have a range of both imperial & metric fittings, & they're quite reasonable, pricewise.' 'Right,' said the voice, 'I'll try going there.' So I replied, 'Not to worry. Have you a message for me? Why do you call to me?' Then the voice sayeth to me, 'Marmalade, Marmalade, the humans aren't listening to me!' And I said, 'Maybe speak a little louder, as some of them are rather deaf.' So the voice said, 'No, I don't think that's the issue. They hear but will not listen.' So I suggested speaking in a human language and not Catanese, but the voice sayeth, 'That's not the problem. Go Marmalade, go and tell them that I have sent you to deliver this message; Woe to Worthing! Woe to

Bournemouth! And woe to Eastbourne! There will be a wailing and gnashing of teeth.' So I replied, 'Probably due to the pensioners not being able to find their false teeth in the dark. Try showing them your light, o Great Being.' And the voice said, 'No that's not the problem. A great tumult is coming to them.' I said, 'A great what?' 'A tumult,' it said. 'What's a tumult, o wise being?' I asked. And it replied, 'Tumult, a turmoil, a troublesome bitterness.' 'Oh,' I said, 'Whence it cometh?' And the voice said, 'Soon, for we have only pencilled it in at the moment and not confirmed the date as such. Yet, soon it will come.'"

"Then what happened?" asked Puddles.

"I don't know, the refrigerator door closed and the voice went."

The catlets adjourned to the house and went upstairs to the study where Marmalade showed Puddles the many books, educating him about cat texts and writings. Marmalade jumped elegantly into the desk, then the top of a bookcase and began to lecture the kitten.

"Now for some inner teachings regarding the mystical arts. There are certain esoteric teachings which were written down, in ancient Catscratch, in the 8th Century by Cedric the Elder. In the 4th book of Cedric, chapter 2, it says, 'Said the master to his disciple, 'If no one is around, can one hear the sound of one tree clapping? And if you could, what would it sound like?' 'What type of tree is it?' asked the disciple. 'Why does it matter?' replied the master. 'Well,' said the disciple, 'A horsechesnut tree haveth nuts on it that would rattle and a conifer hath none so it would be quieter, wouldn't it?' So the master said, 'In this instance it is a cedar tree, alright?' Hence, the disciple pondered these questions a bit then answered, 'I'm not sure for I don't truly understand the questions.' Said the master in exasperation to his disciple, 'There is a knowledge and wisdom that surpasses all understanding.'

And the disciple replied, 'You're not kidding! I don't understand the blooming questions, let alone the wisdom thou dost try to impart. Maybe break it down a bit further for me, if you will.' Alas, the master was forlorn and uttered, 'If in the bowl of milk the moon shineth, pour out the milk and drink only the moon.' Yet the disciple understandeth not and replied, 'Is the milk full cream or semi-skimmed?' 'For heaven's sake! Full cream for it is the best,' replied the master. 'Ah well, I cannot chuck away good milk,' said the disciple, 'For presumably that milk was not cheap; 'tis the very cream of the udder and how can one sup the moon anyway? Surely it is only a reflection.' To wit, the master sayeth, 'You're missing the point; try to empty your mind and consider the conundrum.' Yet, still the disciple failed to understand, so the master considered his student to be a blithering idiot and asked, 'If I have nothing, is this still something?' At which the disciple said, 'Sorry. Now you've totally lost me; maybe ask another, easier riddle so I may understand.' And the master sighed, losing all hope in the student and cast him asunder with a clip around the ear. Upon being struck, the disciple said, "Ah!' And the master thought the student had thus become enlightened, saying, with hope in his voice, 'Do you understand now? 'No,' replied the disciple, 'You actually really hurt me!' 'Sorry,' said the master, 'I did not mean to hurt you.' 'That's okay,' replied the disciple, 'However, the sound of your strike upon my ear soundeth not unlike a cedar tree, without nuts, clapping with one hand in the forest.' The master then rejoiced for the disciple hath become illumined."

After having some food that the humans placed on the kitchen bench, Marmalade began to say goodbye to Puddles. Preparing his young apprentice for the future, he gave him some final advice.

"Now, know this, Puddles. Whatever you put your mind and concentration on, you become and achieve. If you ask the Supreme Cosmic Being for anything, believe it possible by acting as if you have already received it. This is the key to understanding the universe, multiverse, prayer and contemplation.

"Know you have achieved, received and been blessed, and it shall happen. It is this magic that shows itself in the light, in atoms, in everything."

"Like sand? Once you've been in sand it gets ruddy everywhere, man. I always remember my Ma' askin' if I'd been playin' in sand. She'd say, 'You've been playin' in sand again, ain't yer? It's absolutely, ruddy everywhere! What a mess, man! Get yer self out and lick yer self clean,' but sand is really salty and it's horrible when ya gets loadsa it on yer tongue, innit?"

"Yes," smiled Marmalade, in a way that was actually saying, "Shut up!"

"I feel we've moved away from the subject at hand, young Puddles. Where was I? The law of attraction, that's right. Now, one has to realize that the object or objective you seek has already been achieved. Celebrate and be thankful for it before you have received it.

"I recall the tale of Ali the Alley Cat from Alexandria. She would repeat a phrase, 'Miaum, ma, miaum, ma, lahdeelah, miaum, ma,' which means, 'Great Sound of the Universe, Great Sound of the Universe, O, Great love and beloved, Great Sound of the Universe.' And Ali kept singing this mantra all the time. Everyone thought her doolahli-tap, but unperturbed she continued, so much so that the Superior Cosmic Being, manifested itself and visited her. 'Ali,' it said, 'I have heard you and your prayer! Ask for whatever you desire and it shall be granted!' So, Ali, humbled herself and bowed low, saying, "If I am allowed, I would very like a cat themed amusement park, so all kittens and catlets can visit and relax here, play, have fun under the Alexandrian sun!" The Superior Cosmic

Being replied, 'It is a selfless wish and request. However, think of the logistics involved, the materials needed, the amount of litter trays that would be required. Where shall it be placed, this large cat themed amusement park? Where is there space large enough? Maybe there is something else you would like, Ali the Alley Cat...' So Ali turned away and thought about what else she might want, then turned back to the great being saying, 'I wish to understand the humans fully; why they waste so much food, why they talk to us in a high pitched baby-type way, why they tell us off when we bring them presents like birds, mice, rats & shrews; why they continue to use money which seems to be a source of much perturbation, why they watch reality television shows which are truly uninteresting, why they make people celebrities who aren't worth celebrating, why they vote to have idiots lead their countries, why they can't all just get on and be friendly with each other & what ever happened to Noel Edmonds?' Then the Superior Cosmic Being replied to Ali saying, 'Any thoughts on where we could build this amusement park?' Then they discussed how and where to build it. And that's how we got Ikea®.

"Thus, let us learn that what we pray for can be realized, if only we ask, receive and believe. And where 2 or more agree on a request, it shall be done."

Puddles nodded his head in understanding, pondering the words of the teacher.

"Now, I understand that there's been a lot to take in for you, young Puddles, but I intend to return. I shall give unto you this book that I wrote. It contains all the wisdom that I carry in my noggin and more besides. Until I return, read."

"Aye, that I will, marra," said Puddles .

Marmalade walked over to the kitten and placed a reassuring paw on his shoulder, then licked Puddles face and ears.

"Now I bid thee farewell. Until next time, Puddles, adieu..."

Then Marmalade plodded along through the catflap, down the back garden and vanished. Puddles watched the mystic moggy disappear, seeing Marmalade's head look backwards over his shoulder briefly before he leapt up, mysteriously disappearing mid leap. It made the kitten shiver in surprise .

"What a canny cat," he said as went to the windowsill to watch the sun set and moon rise.

"You're not so bad either," whispered a familiar voice. Looking around, he was surprised to see no one, but he did however see the book that had been left and it was called...

FELINE FABLES & MOGGY MORALS.

Now there are lots of things in this veritable universe besides catlets and doglings, like flutterflies and flutterbugs, dandehogs and ladylions, birdies and ballydogs, corpidons and snothogs, burpeesheeps and candybleets, chicklets and froglings, manbugs and moocows, meeces and hollerbats, horsenez and flitty-flights, mothlings and jitternits, helefumps and fishlets, and much more besides, all of whom have their tales to tell...

The Moths.

Now, there was this moth that was not very bright, but like every moth, it loved the light. Every night, it searched for light, whether it be a lamp or the reflected moonlight, but suddenly one dark night, the moth turned his head and got quite a fright.

"Ah!' The moth screamed and other moths who were in sight cried, 'What? What's the matter?' To which the moth pointed with its left wing, 'Over there! Look! A giant, black thing! All dark and monstrous with huge black wings!' The other moths were also afraid, so turned their heads, trying to look away. 'Let us get closer to the lamp light, for the light is bright in this dark night, where monstrous creatures with large, black wings, chase after our furry bodies with wings!' So the moths flew closer to the light, but the first moth, who was not very bright, kept turning around, then screaming, would say, 'The monstrous thing, that's black with wings, chases after us wee little things! Quick, let's gather around the lamp so bright, and hide away from this beast of the night! And how did it, how did it get in to this shed? This vile black creature which we dread?"

"The same way you got in,' said a wise, old duck with a quack. 'By flying in through that big crack, that's up there in the wall through which many an insect also crawls. What is it that frightens you so?'

"The big, black thing with wings, it follows! As we aim for the light, it grows and grows!'

"Well, of course it will,' said the duck. 'If you try to escape, you'll not have much luck!'

"Will it eat us? Will it lure us in for the kill?'

"Oh no, I don't think it will...'

"Then what fate awaits us? Is it worse than death? To be eaten alive, in the beak of death?'

"No,' said the duck. 'No such thing. You'll be pretty safe; there'll be no suffering.'

"So an instant death? To be swatted by some boot wielding person? To such things, we have quite an aversion!'

"Nope. Not that either. No evil comes your way. No swatting, no eating, no stomach for a grave.'

"Then what will happen? What is it we fear?'

"Your own mind, you silly thing, for it's your shadow you fear!'

The moth that was not very bright, but like every moth, loved the light, had let his imagination give him the fear. And the old duck laughed away, 'You're frightened of your own shadow, my dear, and fear only grows in the shadows of imagined ideas."

And as the old duck waddled away, it happened across two rabbits, enjoying the evening sun...

The Two Rabbits.

Merrily they skipped about, until they noticed something rather odd. A larger creature came in to their view, covered in rabbit fur, with some of it floating away in clouds of fluff.

"Skip, skip, skippity hop. Skip, skippity, hop," went the unusual looking animal.

The two rabbits looked at each other, discussing what animal it actually was.

"It's a fox, I'm pretty sure it is."

"Nah, it's a coyote, I think."

"It's definitely a fox, you can tell from the tail between its legs.."

"Looks more like a coyote to me."

Still arguing about it, they went over to the peculiar Coney.

"Excuse me, what are you exactly?"

"I'm a rabbit! Skip, skip, skippity hop. Skip, skippity, hop. See, can't you tell?"

"No, actually, we can't. You look like some sort of dog."

"Well I'm a rabbit! Skip, skip, skippity hop. Skip, skippity, hop."

"The curious creature continued jumping around erratically and announcing its movements. The first rabbit squinted his eyes to try and discern what the animal before him was and the second rabbit was following its movements, also trying to make sense of the curious critter.

"You're a fox! You're a fox in rabbit furs."

"No, I'm a rabbit! See... Skip, skip, skippity hop. Skip, skippity, hop."

"Look mate, one - rabbits aren't as big as you, two - we don't have fluff flying off of us, and three - we don't say 'skip, skip, skippity hop, skip, skippity, hop as we're hopping about!"

"Er, excuse you! I am a rabbit, I'll have you know!"

"You are not! Anyone can see you're a fox in patches of rabbit fur with your tail tucked between your legs and a white bunny-tail has been stuck on your rear end," said the second rabbit. "And you're not doing a very good impression of a rabbit! Anyone can see you are not a rabbit!"

"Ah, but I am! Come closer and you'll see..."

"No chance! We ain't stupid," said the first rabbit.

"Come closer and I can assure you that your eyes will see that I am truly a bunny-rabbit."

The bunnies talked in a hushed manner to each other, and then the second rabbit hopped away.

"Where is she going?" asked the phoney Coney.

"To get the rabbit expert."

"A rabbit expert? You have an expert rabbit?"

"Yes, yes we do."

A few moments later, a noise was heard and something clambered through the tall grass. Suddenly, it stood up and overshadowed the rabbits and bunny impersonator.

"Who is this?"

"The rabbit expert."

"The fox looked up to see a large bear looking downwards at him. Lifting an eyebrow high on its forehead the bear stared at the fox.

"That's not a rabbit expert! That's a bear," said the fox.

"And you're not a bunny-rabbit! You are a fox!"

Then the bear ran towards the fox as it tried to run away.

"I am a rabbit," shouted the fox as it fled away.

"If you're a rabbit, I'll soon find out! Come here and let me look at you!"

"No," said the fox. "I might look like an idiot, talk like an idiot and act like an idiot, but I ain't such an idiot that I don't know when the odds are against me!"

The fox then ran away, narrowly avoiding a slithery snake in its path...

THE SCRUMADUMPALULAH.

It crawled and scuttled about. Feeling peckish, it looked about for something to eat. It slithered around, quietly and happened upon a mouse who was merrily making his way from there to here and here to there. The snake began to lift itself up, ready to strike the mouse, but the little mouse noticed the snake's shadow begin to loom over him.

"Don't eat me!"

"Why ever not? You're nice and lean, not too much fat, and you'll slip quite nicely down my neck. With one gulp you will be gone, a breakfast, lunch and dinner, all in one. You'll be oh, so tasty, in my tum."

"But I'm not a mouse."

"Of course you're a mouse! You have fur, big ears, whiskers for twitching; four legs and a tail. Now let me eat, my stomach is twitching...."

"I'm not a mouse; I'm a er, er, a Scrumadumpalulah."

"A what?"

"A Scrumadumpalulah."

"What's a Scrumadumpalulah?"

"Well, a Scrumadumpalulah looks like a mouse, sounds like a mouse, yet isn't a mouse. If one were to eat a Scrumadumpalulah, they would find it tastes of fish poo and liquorice, with a hint of lavender. If one were to catch a Scrumadumpalulah, they would feel their skin begin to dry up and slide off, because the very touch of a Scrumadumpalulah is fatal to most snakes. Mostly California Rat Snakes."

The snake pulled its neck back sharply.

"I'm a California Rat Snake! Have I touched you; did I touch you yet?"

"No, you didn't. Lucky you!"

"Phew," said the snake. "I've never heard of a Scrumadumpalulah before. Is there anything else I should know about them? Are there lots of them?"

"We're quite a rare breed actually - I'm a Gouty Scrumadumpalulah. The Common Scrumadumpalulah is more commonplace. Now, it's said that if anyone, or thing, helps a Scrumadumpalulah in time of need, the Scrumadumpalulah is obliged to offer some form of reciprocation."

"Like what?"

"Ooo, like turn a stone into a big, tasty rat for a friendly snake..... maybe."

"They're magical, these Scrumadumpalulahs?"

"Not strictly speaking; we're just rather gifted with the alchemy of food."

"Well, is there anything I could do to... How can I help you?"

"Well, I'm in need of a bodyguard, so I don't get eaten on my way home. Or mistaken for a mouse!"

So the rat snake offered its services and made sure the Scrumadumpalulah got home safely. Once at the mouse's, sorry the Scrumadumpalulah's home, the snake slithered near to the furry creature.

"Thank you ever so much for taking care of me. These are treacherous times for Scrumadumpalulahs y'know! Now, as a reward... See that large sandy coloured rock over there? Well, swallow it whole and as it slips down your throat, you'll notice the taste of the bestest tasting, leanest rat you have ever eaten. But swallow it whole mind! Once it is past your ears, let the flavour of the leanest, bestest rat fill your tummy."

So the snake went over as the Scrumadumpalulah, sorry, the mouse went into his home and saw the big sandy rock and swallowed it in one gulp. Once it was in its mouth completely, it let it slip down past his eyes and ears then paused to savour the flavour. However, the taste wasn't very ratty, wasn't very rat but was very salty and very, very sandy. Realising he had been tricked, he tried to spit out the huge sandy rock and took himself away, rather annoyed.

The next night, when the snake came out for its breakfast, lunch and supper, he gathered some friends from around and they went to the home of the Scrumadumpalulah. Knocking hard on the ground above the burrow, an annoyed mouse popped his head up and said, "Oi, what you banging for?"

"Ah," said the rat snake. "Look, it's a Scrumadumpalulah. In fact it's a Gouty Scrumadumpalulah! Actually, look there's a whole family of Scrumadumpalulahs! What favours we shall get if we escort you safely on your nocturnal journeys to find food. Please, allow us to be your bodyguards..."

The mouse and family left the house, smiling happily at the food they would get under the protection of the snakes. But at the end of the journey, the Scrumadumpalulah's tummies were very empty, but the snake's bellies became very, very full.

Now, this had happened for the mice had not kept their wits about them. That's right, their wits, which are very, very important to have about you...

Pet Wits.

Now, do you know what a wit looks like?

Well, they're cute, furry things that are very, very small, about so high and can jump, run and crawl.

They give good advice, so pay heed to when they call, for these furry, little wits have good instincts, that's for sure.

One day I was walking in the town, when a salesman came my way, telling me about his magic potion and how it would make my day. 'It cures 9 out of 10 illnesses and makes you feel good about yourself, so come buy 2 or 3 bottles, as it's good for your health!'

It was at this point I noticed that some of my pets were not around and wondering what to do, I searched everywhere till they were found. And when I found my wits, they gave sound advice, so I put it into action, for they are extremely wise.

Yet, what does a wit sound like? How can someone know how to hear them? They sound similar to this, when you are truly near to them;

In silence there's an inner voice that sounds something like you, so listen to this little, nagging voice that's telling you what to do. If you ever feel that there's ever any doubt, have no fear for you will hear them, as wits tend to shout.

If you ever lose your wits, make sure you go and find them, for when seldom used, it can be rather hard to find them.

When in a battle of wits, they won't let you come to any harm and those people who get injured were relatively unarmed.

If ever you are at your wit's end, give them an extra mile, as gathering up your wits may take a while.

There are two breeds of wits, full wits and halfwits they are named and only people with halfwits ever feel ashamed.

You see, halfwits don't keep their owners faithfully by their side and as they always go missing are even harder to find.

So, keep your wits about you and you'll never be surprised, for only those with halfwits are those who are unwise.

Wits are always helpful, fluffy, cute and kind and if you have your wits about you'll always be of sound mind.

So now you know of wits, I shall explain how they communicate. They often speak in the silence of one's conscience. The interesting thing about them though is that, unlike us, they don't curse or blaspheme and I think we can learn a thing or two from them and maybe use their terms and words rather than using bad language. So here are some of terms used by the wits.

Gummatestrenth - An exclamation, or to pray, for the strength to endure a situation or person.

Lessanid - A person who has made a mistake.

Madjnit - A person who has made a big mistake.

Hugglebucker - One who is being cheeky & rude, either from their mouth or bottom.

Whamhole - An exclamation regarding a frustrating situation or person, as in 'You utter whamhole!' Or 'That's an absolute whamhole!'

Shutterbug - An exclamation at a situation being other than the norm, or going from bad to worse.

Numwub - An endearing term for someone you have affection for, yet persistently makes mistakes.

Compluttering - To stress the severity, intent, or amplify the stress, as in, "You compluttering whamhole!"

Confudgelingnumbug - A term used when one is at their wits end, extremely stressed or annoyed; an exclamation compacting the dilemma verbally.

For example, one might be annoyed by a person that has led them up a particular stream without a certain paddle and say, "Shutterbug! You compluttering madjnit! What do you think you are doing, you numwub?"

Or if one is at the edge of a cliff and there's no bridge and people pursuing them, they may utter, "Confudgelingnumbug! I'm shutterbugged now!"

If someone accidentally shoots you it's possible you may utter, "What you doing you numwub? What kind of whamhole are you?"

Or if you stumble in some animal's faeces, one may exclaim, "Shutterbug!"

Equally, if you are in shutterbug and a posse is behind you and your horse has run away, it would be suitable to say, "You lessanid! Come back here! Gummatestrenth and get back here you compluttering whamhole or I'm shutterbugged! Confudgelingnumbugs!" Yet the horse fails to return.

When encountering a hugglebucker, a shrewd use of language is required as it often entails a battle of wits, hence their vast repertoire of detrimental terms.

And here are some more;

Gurning Ramjacker - Gurning is when someone contorts, pulls a face or expression that uglifies a person's visage. A ramjacker is one who hijacks a ram in order to gain travel to a location not too far away. The combination of the two words implies the person is pulling a less than glamorous facial expression whilst in the throes of an activity.

Flutterbuck - A term used for people who fly in the face of convention.

Rimjawed Gumfluppet - A person who is significantly arrogant in assertions that are wrong and assumes they are always right.

Guppety - To be contrary and doing the opposite of what they mean.

Tadgenuckered - One who is, or the act of being vexed, annoyed or frustrated, as in, "I think they're tadgenuckered over not being able to fix that bucket."

So, if someone you meet has an argument that is clearly wrong and pulls faces at your replies and opinions, you might say, "Oh, you guppety, rimjawed, gumfluppet! Stop being a gurning ramjacker, you're tadgenuckering me, you utter flutterbuck!"

My personal favourite expression is 'compluttering whamhole,' as we meet many of them in our daily lives, yet inasmuch as it is seen as an insult, it is neither blasphemous, cursing or crude.

Someone who had her wits about her was an Alpaca called, Anna, who wandered over the mountains, visiting here, anywhere and there. She was a bit of an adventurer, being curious about what was beyond the next hill, the next mountain...

The Drama Llamas.

One very late night, she heard something going on, something that she'd never heard before. It sounded like a lot of moaning and wailing. Her inquisitive nature prompted her to have a look at what was going on.

"Ohhhh - uhhhh - ohhhh."

"Whatever are you doing?"

"Ssshhh - were calling the morning sun!"

"What?"

"We summoning the sun! Sshh," said a llama, then turned back to join the others.

The moaning continued, until the right amount of repetitions were completed.

"What on earth are you doing?" asked Anna.

An older llama turned to the alpaca and explained what was going on.

"We are summoning the sun. We do so each morning, making sure the sun rises for the day. If we don't, the sun will not rise."

"Er, why?"

"Because we wouldn't have summoned it! Hence the need for the summoning song."

Anna thought about it then said, "Well, I've never heard anyone summoning the sun before; normally it just pops up."

"Aha! But only because we sing the song!"

"And before llamas sung the song, how did the sun rise?"

"The great, wise Alma created the sun for those who cried out for light, so they may be drawn from the dark despair."

"I see. So why didn't Alma just leave it in the sky?"

"So that we would always know to depend on the summoning. Hence, we sing the summoning song to awaken the sun."

"Oh, right! Seems a bit odd though.'

Once the llamas had finished singing, the chief llama made a shrill noise and said, "Fetch forth the sacred stone of dawn..."

Another llama brought to the group a small bluish stone.

"Behold, the sacred stone of dawn. Let us place it upon the sacred corn bed."

"Awallah, neck zutong drachk-ker-ker," cried the llamas.

"Why's the stone sacred?"

"Because it is."

"But why? How is it sacred?"

"Because I was told it was. Now place it on the bigger stone, on the corn bed then turn around three times & say the words, Morga-morga-morg-Aha!."

"What does that do?"

"What does what do?"

"The stone. What does it do?"

"It helps in the summoning..."

"Of the dawn?"

"Yes, the summoning of the dawn! Now bring forth the seal so the sun can break from the shackles of night..."

The mangy old seal was brought before the gathering and placed on the stone.

"Behold the sacred seal of Ruppadum, behold the blessed chalice, behold the sacred spitting dish."

A procession proceeded to bring out a rusty cup and a wooden dish that had seen better days.

"Now, let us welcome the dawn! Where-e're-ego-goes-we-gogo-where-ego-goes! Let us all sing..."

Anna watched the llamas singing raucously.

"Where-e're-ego-goes-we-gogo-where-ego-goes!"

"Where-e're-ego-goes-we-gogo-where-ego-goes! Come on, put some effort into it! Where-e're-ego-goes-we-gogo-where-ego-goes! Where-e're-ego-goes-we-gogo-where-ego-goes!"

However, the sun had still not emerged.

The chief llama halted proceedings.

"It's not working, we need to do more!!! And begin the wailing..."

The llamas began singing once more and a portion of them wailed loudly, sobbing wildly and feigning sorrow.

"Where-e're-ego-goes-we-gogo-where-ego-goes! Come on, come on, put some effort into it! More!! Where-e're-ego-goes-we-gogo-where-ego-goes! Where-e're-ego-goes-we-gogo-where-ego-goes!"

Yet still the sun had not arisen. It was if the sun was not listening.

"There must be something wrong, for the sun it doth not riseth," said the chief. "Let us begin the Headnuggin!!!"

At once, the llamas started banging their heads on each other, rocks, anything nearby, as well as wailing and singing their song, "Where-e're-ego-goes-we-gogo-where-ego-goes! Where-e're-ego-goes-we-gogo-where-ego-goes! Where-e're-ego-goes-we-gogo-where-ego-goes!"

Anna was aghast at the llamas and their activity.

"You do realize nothing you can do can make the sun come up?"

"Of course there is! We must have upset or annoyed the sun, so we must appease it. I need a willing volunteer to jump into the chasm of despair. Who will it be?"

The suddenly sheepish llamas backed up.

"Who volunteers to jump into the chasm of despair? Is it you, André? Or you, Selma? Or maybe, Juan?"

"You want me? To jump? Into the chasm of..."

"The chasm of despair!"

"Sounds a bit dangerous," said Juan.

"We need someone, fearless, bold and brave."

"How about, Iago? He's braver than me..."

Iago's face turned to stone.

"I'm not brave, or bold. Juan is definitely fearless, choose him."

And an argument broke out between them regarding who was bolder and fearless. That was until Anna the Alpaca butted in.

"Look, no one needs to jump into a chasm! No one needs to cry, sing, turn around 3 times and spit into a dish. You're all daft. Neither does anyone need to use a sacred stone, a bed of corn or sing a stupid song."

The chief llama looked bemused.

"No?"

"No. Can you change the seasons? Command the tide to come in sooner?"

"Er, well, er... No."

"Then how can you make the sun rise?"

The chief llama appeared dismayed. Anna then proceeded to explain how the moon spins around the earth, the Earth moves around the sun and how we have a morning, evening and night.

The llama listened, but was not convinced, so Anna asked him to sit with her and watch what happens. And as the sun emerged on the horizon, the llama finally understood. In a moment of realisation, it dawned on him. Anna the Alpaca then wandered off over the next mountain, to see what was over there and what she saw was the smallest of persons that have ever been, who had an ambition and a dream.

SMALL MAN STAN.

This little man, who we shall call, Stan, had a problem and a plan; "This tree is in my view and I need to move it, so what to do...My home is perfect, just right and neat, yet this tree needs to be moved which shall be quite a feat!"

So little man, Stan, decided to see how he might move the tree and went to the wise woman, Ava, who it turns out you see, owed him more than a favour, or three. Upon his arrival at her den, she cried out, "Hello, Stan! I've been awaiting the pleasure of meeting you, for it's been a long time, of this it's true. Tell me, what is it you are after?"

"Good morrow to you," said Stan to Ava. "I am actually asking after a favour. Please come with me and you'll see the calamity, for the vista from my home which I see, is blocked by a very large, olden tree."

"A tree? It blocks your view? Uhm, what shall you do?"

"Move it," said Stan in the swift retort, as Ava searched for a solution within her thoughts.

"Come let us go to your abode and show to me this tree that obscures your view and then we'll discover to do!"

So off they went down the road, through the village and further they strode; up the track, behind the back of the farmer's barn, then further still through a field, until they arrived at Stanley's home.

"Uhm, yes, it's indeed a calamity, to have one's view obscured by a tree. Tell me, could you not move your house, nearer to the field where lives the grouse?"

"Move my home?"

"No, build a new house."

"And start from scratch? And live next to the grouse? No, I don't want to move. 'Tis only my view I need to improve!"

"But this tree's been here for an eternity! Why can't you let it be? You'd be better off relocating your home. And you should have thought of this a long time ago! Why build a home where such fenestration is obscured by such large vegetation? It would have been easier to build a home in a more suitable place, that has a nice view and grants nature the grace, to be as it needs to be, and not having to relocate this tree!"

And in these words Stan did think, pondering Ava's remarks as he poured two drinks.

"There is only one solution," said Ava who was duty bound to her favour, "You need the magic flower, for only this has the power, to relocate such a tree, this resolving your calamity."

"Magic flower," said Stan, "Where is this pray, tell?"

"In the furthest field where you can just about hear the church bell. There it resides in a curious meadow, hallowed by presence of a mystical fellow. Eustace is what he prefers to be called, but he is no idiot, so don't be fooled, for an idiot is what he appears to be, but his flower's magic can move your tree."

So Stan set off, trudging through field and meadow, as the six o'clock bell began to hollow. As its peel became very hard to hear, Stan saw Eustace begin to appear.

"What do you want," asked the strange chap. "For I'm about to take my morning nap."

"At 6 in the evening, you have a morning nap?"

"I got up late, so what's wrong with that?"

"I would like to borrow the magic flower, for I've heard of its power."

"I'm off to bed; come back in an hour!"

"I have travelled far, from the village of Tauw. Can I not just borrow it now?"

"Oh, I don't know, as I'm late for my nap! Can't you just come on back?"

After taking some convincing, Eustace gave in to Stan's insisting and led him towards the magic flower, the one that had the mystic power. Being led towards a small patch, Stan saw eight flowers in all, all of which matched.

"Which one is it? They all look the same."

"Take your pick, they are all the same!"

"So all eight are blessed with magical powers?"

"That might be right, but only one is the right flower."

"But which one? Is this a game?"

"Ah, here come on, I'll show how they're not all the same."

So Eustace plucked out the singular flower, the one that had all the mystic powers, then placed it in the hand of Stan, who marched off home to hatch his plan. However, Stan had to pay heed to the advice of Eustace, so the plant would not be rendered useless. The rules of the magic plant are:

- Be grateful in advance and give lots of thanks to the plant,

- Only use positive language, no mights or maybes; no, "I wonder ifs..." nor " Do you understand me?

- Know that of what you have asked, has already come to pass,

- And last of all, use it only for right reasons, not for gain or selfish, greedy ambition.

These 3, or 4, rules must be obeyed, and never must its trust be betrayed. On these things, Eustace insisted and as Small Man Stan wandered off, his voice persisted, "Be grateful, use language positively, know that it's already happened and don't be greedy!" Thus, reciting the rules, Stan made away to the village of Tauw, all the while remembering how to, be positive, know that it's already occurred, be thankful with every positive word.

Ava was on the horizon and could be seen, sizing up the enormous tree. With a hand on her chin, her head shaking in thought, talking to herself, as if she really ought to be somewhere else, doing other things, not idly waiting for Stan, among other things. She could be reading, or cooking her tea, not trying to move an almighty tree. She could be having a biscuit, or a cake, writing recipes to later bake; or playing a game with her frog, or reciting her wisdom to both human and dog, both of whom needed her advices, as folly followed both around leading them in to vices, that may seem quite tame to many, but to others cost more than a penny. And freely she gave her wise words, free of cost to anyone who heard; pigeons, stoats, cats and birds, all needed wisdom in words, as did horses, men, women and mice, snakes, squirrels, leeches and woodlice.

Then arrived at the tree did he, the Small Stan Man with a flower of mystery. Ava glanced at the plant and, having given a cautionary glance, sized up the unassuming flower, head, leaf and stalk, wondering where resideth its power. With a smile long and wide, small Stan laid the plant aside and with a big inhalation, begun his proclamation.

"Oh, great and wonderful tree, thank you for your oxygen and shade, but I'm afraid that you're in my way. I really hope you wouldn't mind if you would move to the side, so I can see the lake from where I reside."

Nothing happened .

"Was there, by any chance, any instructions for the plant?" asked Ava.

"Yes, there were: be grateful, use language positively and know that it's happened already!"

Stan thought for a while, a grin now replacing his smile.

"Dear tree, Thank you for your photosynthesis, your leaves and shade, and nutty business. I wonder if you'd be ever so kind and please move to one side."

Ava looked in to the air and noticed the tree was still there.

"I think the key to the problem, is knowing that it has already happened. So try thanking the tree for its moving in advance, believing it has already moved at once!"

"Right... O, wonderful, majestic tree, thanks for moving to the left so I can see the sea."

At once the tree moved to the left, leaving them aghast, for they'd witnessed the moving of a humongous plant. Now, wondering what else the flower could do, Stan also asked for his house to move.

"You wonderful logs that make my building, thank you in advance for moving a little more towards the right so I can see the most wonderful sight of the sea and the shore from my window and my door."

At once, the wooden home moved, making the vista much improved. Then dancing around with glee, Small Man Stan and Ava were so happy. However, just as they were celebrating, they heard a voice puffing and panting. Behold,

Eustace stood before them, puffing and panting, trying to warn them.

"I made a mistake, you've got the wrong flower; that ain't the one with the power! Try this one here, that looks like a daisy. Sorry 'bout this, for my memory's hazy..."

"But how can this be?" said Ava, "Can't you see? Now Stan has a clear view of the sea?"

And a stunned silence befell them, leaving each one dumb, wondering what really had been done. Then Ava, being ever so wise, discerned what had happened and opened their eyes.

"My dears, this enigma can only be embraced by understanding, Stan, had a little faith. By moving the home and the tree, faith has revealed to all its true mystery."

Magnum O'Puss.

Now, pay attention! Are you listening? No. Well, heed Marmalade's words, for my next tale will help you to understand the ways the Supreme Cosmic Being assists us. So, let us begin...

In a certain country, at a certain time, at a particular location, that being the rotting branch of a tree reaching out over the rapids of a river, a certain cat, called Magnus, made his way across the river. I don't know how he quite got there, maybe he was chasing some chickens, or mice, or maybe he was taking in the lovely, panoramic view... Anyway, Magnus, happened to think about crossing the river. As you know, us catlets dislike water somewhat, thus Magnus finds himself walking over the river by virtue of a branch, albeit a rotten one. Why a rotten one, I don't know, he should have done some reconnaissance first, I feel, but alas he had not and Magnus broached the significantly large branch so to traverse the river wild. He was about halfway across when he noticed that the branch was not as sturdy as first he thought .

'Oh,' he thinks, 'I might slip and fall to my doom from atop this rotten wood. I know what I shall do, I shall call upon the Supreme Cosmic Being so he can come and save me.'

And thus, Magnus begins supplicate the SCB. For ages he is wailing and moaning, sounding like a caterwauling banshee, until a bear-cub passes by.

'Hello, is that you making that awful racket?' asks the bear-cub.

'Yes,' says Magnus, 'I have broached this river on this dodgy plank and I don't think it can take my weight.'

'I see,' says the bear. 'I'll break a large tree for you so it falls and bridges the river, then you can cross safely.'

However, Magnus protested, 'No, no, no. There is no need for the Supreme Cosmic Being shall save me. I have been petitioning him for his assistance and I'm sure he will save me.'

'Are you absolutely sure?' asks the bear cub.

'No, I'll be alright, but thanks ever so much for stopping and offering to help.'

'You're most welcome!' says the bear.

And thus, the bear went away, going about his business. Magnus, began to tentatively move onward on the rotten branch, looming over the foamy rapids. 'Those rocks look nasty and very sharp,' he thought. However, as he progressed, the branch began to make a snapping sound and he stopped, robustly in his tracks. Once more he placated the Supreme Cosmic Being for assistance from the predicament and the wailing, crying and praying began once more.

'Who dost make that bloomin' row?' asked a vexed dog , who was a-wandering in the direction of the river. 'You doth pollute my ears with that raucous carry-on!'

Magnus apologised for the noise, begging a question from the dog, 'Is everything okay?'

And Magnus replied explaining his predicament. The dog at once offered assistance, saying, 'Jump on my back as I swim through the water and I shall ferry you to t'other side and the bank.'

Yet, Magnus declined the canine's assistance, saying, 'There is no need, for the Supreme Cosmic Being shall save me. I have been petitioning him for his assistance and I'm sure he will save me.'

'You sure?' quizzed the dog.

'Yes, the Supreme Cosmic Being has got my back, dude.'

The dog was most perplexed but sallied forth to do his dog doo-doo by a suitable lava-tree. Did you see what I did there? Did you like it? Lava-tree? Lavatory, lava-tree? Oh, there's no amusing some people! Anyway, our puss with a problem remained on the branch, beseeching and imploring the Supreme Cosmic Being to come to his aid. The branch was becoming ever so creaky and about to give to the strain of the cat's weight, when a large duck paddled below the pussycat and began to trod water (or is it trud? Or treaded maybe?! Anyway...) as it gazed at the water spraying up at the now moist moggy.

'Hello? Are you okay up there?' said the duck. 'You seem to be in a bit of a pickle. Quickly, climb on to my back and I shall take you to the bank.'

But yet again, Magnus replied, 'There is no need, for the Supreme Cosmic Being shall save me. I have been petitioning him for his assistance and I'm sure he will save me. He's very good like that!'

And the ducky said, 'Come on, quickly, for the branch is about to give up its ghost and snap, for sure.'

'No, I best not. I am a cat, y'know! I eat ducks, usually.'

'Well surely you can control your urges temporarily, can't you?'

'No, I'm not that disciplined actually.'

'Well, you should be, in case of such circumstances such as these! Now hurry and jump on my back at once!'

And so Magnus magnificently jumped on to the duck's back and they paddled downstream. Whilst they made their way to a suitable piece of shoreline so the cat could alight from the drake, Magnus couldn't stop thinking of red-currant jelly and how well it went with duck meat and needless to say, he ate the duck in midstream. The duck said, 'What are you doing?'

And Magnus said, 'I'm sorry, but I did warn you, it's in my nature, and I'm a bit peckish after all that perturbation!'

Thus, alas the duck was eaten, for he was plump breasted and indeed delicious, sans red-currant jelly. So Magnus, who could not swim, drowned in the rapid waters of the river. When his soul migrated to cat heaven, he approached the Supreme Cosmic Being and said, 'Forgive me for asking, O Supreme Being, but I was rather wondering what happened down there, on that branch, over that river, where I was trying to dodge the whole not-dying-yet type thing. I was rather hoping you'd save me.'

The SCB looked at Magnus rather amazed and said, 'Well, I did try; I sent a bear-cub, a dog and then a rather strong duck, but you ate him!'

And here endeth the lesson. So be aware of how the almighty can and does help. For there are times when, it hath no paws but ours to help with, hath no ears but ours to hear with and no mouth but ours to speak with. Oh, and try not to eat those who assist you.

BATTITUDE.

Far away across the meadow, not too far from Stan, two young she-bats were fighting, again, in the way that sisters do when they share the same belfry.

"It's mine!"

"No, it's mine! I found it first! "

"It's mine! I saw it first!"

"Well I had hold of it first!"

Then one sister hit the other.

"Hold on there! Whoah! What are you fighting for?" asked Papa-Bat.

"She hit me!"

"No, you hit me!"

"Okay. Back up now! You shouldn't hit your sister and you shouldn't fight either! Now say you're sorry, both of you."

"Sorry!"

"Yeah, well I'm sorry too... in your dreams!"

The dad pulled them apart before they could start fighting again.

"If you say sorry, you gotta say it as you mean it and have the attitude that a bat must have, that of battitude."

"What's battitude?"

"Battitude is the attitude that a bat must have. It's about having the right attitude when you're doing something."

"What do you mean?"

"Well," said the Papa-bat as he began to sing.

"When you're doin' what you do

You gotta check your attitude

And remember how'd you'd do it

If you were doin' it for you.

"So if what you're doin' is

Not in the right mood,

Just remember how'd you'd do it

If you were doin' it for you.

"How would you say it

If you were sayin' it to you?

So listen to how you'd say it

And with the right attitude.

Just remember how'd you'd talk

If you were sayin' to you.

And do everything in the way

That you'd have it done to you.

"If you do your best

You got nothin' else to prove

So what you doin'?

What you provin'?

Why you provin' it and to whom?

"And if you're in a fight

You must resist the attitude,

Know you cannot hit them

Yes, it's the smartest, hardest move.

"So remember how'd you'd do it

If you were doin' it for you.

Just remember how'd you'd do it

If you were doin' it for you.

Remember how'd you'd do it

If you were doin' it for you.

Just remember how'd you'd do it

If you were doin' it for you.

"Don't have a bad attitude

Or do things in a mood.

Do it positively with a smile

For this is true Battitude.

Remember how'd you'd do it

If you were doin' it for you.

And if you do it like this

It keeps you in the right mood.

So remember how'd you'd do it

If you were doin' it for you,

For doing it like this means

you have true Battitude."

AFTER BERNIE. (FOR SIAN)

Across the meadow, away from the church, there was a large pond, which animals used to drink from. The world above the water was much different to that below, where froglings, fishlets and other things live, like beetles...

From time to time, the beetles gathered under the water lily to see others climb up. They wondered why beetles had this proclivity, to suddenly climb the stem of a lily and one beetle in particular, Bernie, seemed very intrigued.

"Why is it that they want to climb the stem? I would love to know."

"Well, I heard tell that they travel to Heaven," said Betty.

"Heaven? Heaven is at the top of the stem of this lily? How would anyone know? Has anyone come back to say this is so?"

"I don't know, but it's apparently so."

"Well, I have no inclination to climb that stem and I shan't either! Never, ever."

Bernie seemed so defiant and determined that he would never want to climb anything, let alone the stem of a lily. Betty told him other tales also, about the flowers above the water that others had mentioned, about another world being up there and about it being like heaven. Yet Bernie seemed content under the water, knowing his place and safe in what he knew. That was until one day, when he felt somewhat different.

"I wonder what's up there?"

"I thought such things didn't interest you," said Betty.

"Well, they don't ... but..... I have this urge, this feeling that... Oh, I can't resist! I need to climb up there and see for myself."

"Becoming inquisitive are we?"

"No, but something inside me needs to climb up there..."

"Well, Bernie, once you have climbed up there, come back and tell me what it's like. Tell me if Heaven is as wonderful as it sounds. Promise me?"

"I will," said Bernie. "I most surely will."

So up Bernie went, climbing up the stem. It was a long climb for such a small beetle, but eventually he got there and then and made his way to the topside of the water lily. The climbing had taken all his energy out of him and being so tired, he decided to rest.

When he woke up, he felt different... somehow. He felt bigger. He felt taller. He felt like he had wings and when he looked, he did! He had wonderful wings and excitedly began to fly about. Then he realised, he had become a Dragonfly!

"Wow, this really is heaven," said Bernie, as he flew all about, up and down the river. And then he remembered his promise to Betty, to go back and tell her about what was up here, in Heaven. Looking downward, he was about to dive when a Damselfly came to him.

"No, you must not dive in the water, it will damage your wings and you will not be able to fly back through the surface of the water!"

"But I told my friend that I'd go back and tell her what is up here."

"You can't, I'm sorry but you can't."

Feeling sad at breaking his promise, he looked at the water and thought of Betty waiting for him. So he flew gently down and hovered over the water.

Betty, who had been looking upward expectantly, decided to start climbing the stem, to see if she could catch a glimpse of Heaven. She didn't have quite the strength yet to reach the lily, so had to stop, gasping for breath. Deciding to make her way back down, she looked up longingly before her descent and she noticed something, someone above the water, hovering. She tried hard to see what it was but couldn't quite make out what it was.

Seeing Betty under the surface of the water, Bernie flew a little lower still and hovered for a moment, smiled, then flew off to explore Heaven. He knew one day that Betty would also have that urge, that strength and curiosity, to climb the lily stem and venture to the top side, to rest beside the lily and gain her wings.

So Bernie flew to and fro across the heavens, high above the meadow, over the hills, to far away and even beyond the dunes...

Two Dragons.

Over the hills, far away beyond the dunes, in a very dark cave, lived a dragon named, Ralph. Now, Ralph is not your typical dragon; he has two massive, leathery wings, two legs, two hands, two eyes, two nostrils for breathing out smoke, one mouth and the longest tongue you ever did see, but he is the shyest, nervous, most timid dragon you will ever meet. Ralph lived alone in the cave which looked out over the great lake and nearby meadows where lots of lovely sheep lived. Ralph would often go and chat with the sheep and just generally chill out with them. More often than not, you can find Ralph hangin' out with his homeboy, Lammy and his crew, Boo, Elijah and Cheese.

One day, Ralph was with the gang, just doin' what they do in their own sheepish way.

"Wassup, Ralphy? How's it goin'?" said Lammy.

"I is good, bro. Ima hang out with yous, as there ain't much goin' down dude."

"That's fine, bro. Just chill."

And as they just chilled, what you would expect to happen, didn't. Another dragon flew overhead, lookin' fly, then landed in the pastures green, noticing a dragon chillin' with the sheep

"What are you doin' hangin' out wid these fools? Don't yer know you're a dragon? Dragons don't hang out with no lamb! No. Dragons hang out wid other dragons and eat those sheep."

Nervously, Ralph looked at the other dragon, observing the red, scaly, cool lookin' dude with crimson wings. After observing the visitor, he pulled back slightly.

"Ima hangin' wid my crew. Whoid you?"

"They call me, Drax. What you doin' hangin' out with the lamb, bro'?"

"They my friends, Lammy, Boo, Elijah and Cheese."

"I bet they taste good! You tasted that lamb before?"

"I don't eat no sheep! These are my homies!"

"I got this, bro," said Lammy. "Why don't you jus' move along now, or I'll have you whacked."

"You whack me?" chuckled Drax. "How some dumb lamb like you gonna whack my meat? You ain't even the same size as me. In fact I could get you in my claw and tear your head clean off in a second! Yer feel me?"

"I'd like to see you try, hugglebucker! We da meanest hugglebucker sheep you ever gonna meet!"

"Says who?"

"Says us, fool! Why don't you make your way home, Drax or I'll have my boy, Ralphy, tear you in two."

"Ah, I see. Tha only reason you lambs are so mean is on account of this here sheep lovin' hugglebucker! I bet you ain't so tough when Ralph ain't wid yer."

Ralph was very nervous and trying not to let it show, leaving all the talking to Lammy. As things got heated, Boo and Cheese drew closer to Lammy's shoulders, making real moody looks on their faces and acting like they were carrying guns under their fur. Elijah hung back next to Ralph, looking real mean and threatening.

Ralph quietly talked to Elijah, voicing his concerns.

"Eli, this is gettin' kinda tense."

"Don't stress, bro. If anythin' goes down, just get behind me and breathe fire at this hugglebucker, okay?"

"Okay. So get behind you and smoke this hugglebucker."

"Yea."

Meanwhile, Drax was talking with Lammy, trading insults and assuming that he was some kind of fool, as the sheep was over confident. Drax thought that it would be a different situation altogether if Ralph was not present. Also, the other sheep were approaching to see what was happening.

"What gives you such confidence that you think you can speak to me this way?"

"I tell you why," started Lammy. "This here land, is the valley of the shadow of death and when Ralph here arises, you will see the shadow of death upon thee, as he flies over then straight at you, ready to tear your head clean off yer shoulders."

"And if there no dragon, what you'd be doin'?"

"If there were no dragon around here, I'd still be warnin' yer, as there's more lamb than dragon 'round these parts. Remember, everywhere that you go there's always someone watchin'. Us sheep are everywhere and everywhere that you go I got lamb that I know, who got lamb that they know, so I suggest you lay low[1]."

Drax paused and looked at the mass of sheep approaching.

"You some bad ass, hugglebucker sheep! I respect that. What say we keep da peace? I'm cool wid it. Hey, Ralph, you mind if I hang wid you and your crew some time?"

---

[1] Paraphrased from 'The Watcher' by Dr. Dre.

Ralph looked around. Lammy nodded his head. Cheese nodded his, then Boo and Elijah.

"Yea, that's cool," said Ralph. "You come hang out wid us."

"Cool. You some mighty b-aaad ass sheep. Ain't no one messin' wid yous! Let alone that dragon! I like yer tribe, Lammy. Respect."

And with that, Drax flew away.

"Wow, I was so frightened," said Ralphy. "You were brilliant, Lammy."

"You were frightened? I was absolutely brickin' it, dude! At least there'll be plenty manure for the near future! Sheeesh!"

So, Drax flew high and over the dunes to a sandy town, near to Pity called, Emnity, where two elderly men were bickering...

A Difference of Opinion.

They were always at odds with each other. One was called Josiah, the other was named Rock. Now one day they happened upon a character from a sign in the road; Josiah was crossing from west to east across Main Street, whereas Rock was crossing from east to west. Both stopped and looked at it. Obviously, there was a sign somewhere now devoid of this particular character whether it be a letter or a number. Anyway, Rock stares at the character and says, "Someone's lost a number 9."

"You stupid old fool," says Josiah, "That's a number 6."

"That ain't no number 6, it's a 9!"

"It ain't a 9, it's a 6, I'm tellin' yer! Either that or it's a b."

"A bee, that ain't a bee, a bee is a buzzin' thing!"

"No, it's a b, the letter b, yer eejit!"

"No it ain't! It's a number 9 or maybe a q."

"A q?"

"Yep a q without the serif."

"A sheriff? I ain't seen a sheriff with a q - a badge maybe, a badge with a star on. Only time I see a sheriff with a queue is when there's been high periods of localised crime."

"No, a serif!"

"Seraphim? Like an angel or summat?"

"No, a serif; one of those curly things that are on letters."

"D'ya mean a seal?"

"I'm not talking about Lucille! Don't bring her I'm to this! Is nuthin' to do with Lucille! I'm talking 'bout a serif; that there is a q without a serif, or a number 9. "

"You insane, yer shabby, old goat? That there is a 6, anyone would say that, 'coz anyone can see it, yer stupid old fool!"

"Who you callin' an ol' fool? That there is a 9, or a letter q. You stupid, dumb son of a gun!"

"Now don't be callin' me, or I'll strike you with my walkin' stick."

"Yeah?"

"Yeah!"

"Yeah!! Well if you strike me, I'll take that there number 9 and whip yer wid it!!!"

"Well you won't be able to, 'coz there ain't no number 9, there's only a number 6. Your just too senile to see it you darn crazy old goat."

"It's a 9!"

" 6 . "

"9."

" 6. "

"9 ."

" 6!!!! "

Now the retired judge could hear them arguing and went over to Josiah and Rock.

"Whoah! What is happening here? Are you arguing over this fragment of signage?"

"Yep. Sure am, Dexter! This here eejit, Mr Josiah Fancy-pants Wilson thinks that this is a 6 or possibly a letter b. But as you can see, Dexter, it quite clearly is a 9 or a q sans serif!"

"It's a 6, gosh darn it!"

"Whoah, whoah there fellas," said the judge. "I think this needs some arbitration. So, let's think; you, Rock, contest that this character is a 9, or possibly a q without a serif. Whereas you, Josiah, thinks it to be a 6, correct?"

"Or a b, the letter b, not a buzzin' thing!"

"Or a letter b. Okay. Now have either of you thought that you could both be right, or both be wrong?"

"Nope."

"Noh sir-ee."

"Well I contest that this is possibly a letter or a number, this I can conclude. So, arguably you're both correct."

A man in a set of overalls approached the old men and the judge then bent down and picked up his lost letter, or number. Rock looked at the man. Josiah glared at the man. Judge Dexter said, "Would you be so kind as to resolve an argument? Is this character a number of a letter?"

"It's a letter, actually," said the man.

"And what letter is it, pray tell?"

"It's a P. It must've dropped off when I carried the sign across the road."

The man walked away carrying his P. Josiah grumbled. Rock looked with discontent.

"So you were both wrong! How's about that?" said the Judge.

"Well, I was closest," said Rock. "A q is closer to a p ain't it?"

"No, theoretically, I won, 'coz from my angle it would have been a b, and not some darn buzzin' thing! For what is a b but p upside down!"

"Fellas, fellas," said the Judge , calming them down. "Face facts, you both wrong. Maybe next time you might try seeing things from one another's perspective, eh?"

Now, it seemed like the birds were laughing at the two old hoots, but they weren't. They were just flying about near the edgelands of town.

Two Jackdaws.

They both lived in strongest tree & both of them were mothers and had young in their nests. One night, as they flew off to find food for their children, a strong wind arose.

The wind was strong and blew even the strongest trees to and fro. In the two nests the younglings awaited anxiously for their mothers return. Looking for the mothers return, one chick edged to the top of the nest and looked out. In the other nest, a chick heard the chirrups and climbed to the top of its nest to see who was making the noise and to also look for its mother flying homeward. As both the little birds looked for their mothers, the wind grew even stronger. Then one of the young slipped and hung on to the nest by its beak, grasping desperately. Upon seeing this, the chick in the other nest gasped in shock and the wind then nudged the young bird off the nest and it also grasped a twig so it would not fall.

When the mothers returned, each saw their babies hanging on for dear life. The first mother called out, "Hang on," whilst the other said, "Don't fall!" And they continued to call out to their young. Then a sudden gust of wind caught the branches. The child who was told to "hold on," flapped its little wings and was thrown into its nest. The other who was told, "Don't fall," fell. As it tumbled down and round, down and around, it flapped its little wings, but it was not enough to make it fly. The mother, luckily, caught her chick in her claw as she flew to save it.

After she placed her baby back in the nest, she spoke to the other jackdaw.
"Why did you not fly up to save your chick?"
"Why? Well, I told my child to 'hold on,' and it did. However, you told yours, 'Don't fall,' yet it did. And that is why you had to fly up and save it. You should be careful of what you say, for from your words come reactions whereas others become

actions."

All the commotion has caused a child to stir, who lived in a house nearby to the edgelands. She wasn't sure if what disturbed her, whether it be a dream, the birds or something else, but she was sure that there was something there with her; a presence lurking in the dim light of night, somewhere in the house...

Mary's Nightmare.

Along the dark, dark corridor came the fearless creature, venturing down the stairs, the shadows hiding it hideous features. It crept and crawled along the hall and along to get young Mary, emerging from the darkness, looking mean, rough and hairy. In her fright she awoke to turn on the light and see no creature there, for it was only in her dream that she'd had the scare.

The very next night the same thing happened, again in her dreams, the creature stalked her about the house trying to get a scream. And again the night after, and after that again, the creature roamed about the house trying raise a shout. Then one night, Mary had an idea, to see if there was a light-switch or a table lamp near. So when along the dark, dark corridor did come the fearless creature, venturing down the stairs, the shadows hiding it hideous features, it crept and crawled along the hall to try and get young Mary, emerging from the darkness, looking mean, rough and hairy; it drew closer and closer, closer and closer still, closer, closer and ever closer and that was until- she could feel its breath then scared it half to death, with such a fright, for Mary had reached out her hand and swiftly switched on the light.

"What's the matter? What's wrong?" asked the ugly thing. And Mary asked, "What are you doing every night here inside my dreams?"

"Well how on earth should I know? For this is your imagination!"

"I know," said Mary. "But I never expected to see such an abomination!"

"Well that's not very nice, is it! I never asked to be in your dream! It's for you to decide what's going on inside the depths of your dreams."

"Oh," said Mary. "I never thought of this. I do apologise, for now I realise, you represent the things I fear and miss."

"Well, I'll miss you too," said the creature, "for I enjoyed our time playing hide and seek in your mind. Maybe we could play another game, maybe some other time?"

"I'd like that," said Mary, with a cautious smile.

Some years later, the creature re-appeared to play seek'n'hide. And they talked & talked inside her dream where her hopes and fears reside.

THE "TEXTUS KATTUS EX HONORIA.

Recently, I, Marmalade, rediscovered the lost texts ascribed to the late, great Honoria, who is fondly known as the Queen of Catlets. So naturally I, being of the literary, learned kind of cat, transliterated the texts from ancient Catanese for a more contemporary tongue. One might say that some things get lost in translation, but I pray that this hasn't happened. Anyway, let me read to you the Textus Kattus.

<u>Textus Kattus.</u>

I, Honoria of Shilbottle, am humbled by you, dear reader, taking time to read the words of wisdom given unto me. As thee gathers thy wits about thee, may I make glorious the words as if they be an unction upon thy very soul.

Thus, verily, I say unto you, be kind to one another and not like the bitch down Sycamore Lane (*NB: she is referring to a female catlet and not being offensive*) who is a right little strumpet, and leadeth masculine catlets astray, and maketh a profit for her own (*NB: actually, I think she is being offensive; apologies*). No, neither be unkind or over-familiar. Be a friend, a comfort to one another, helpful and compassionate. Yet don't be aloof, nor a botheration to your neighbour by frequenting their establishment too often. No, get it just right. Nip over for a cup of tea, or milk, and be sociable lest you become a foreigner to them.

Extendeth your paws to be helpful to catlets, doglings and all living things, be it mice, spiders, moths, flies, daddy-long-legs, caterpillars, birds, insects, (*NB: she goes on a bit here to establish that all things are worthy of compassion*) worms, lady-bugs, cockroaches, those things that look like spiders but aren't, having wings and lots of legs; rats, bats, hats, anything that rhymes with cat, tulips, onions, trees, plants, any growing thing. (*NB: I'll stop here as I think you have the gist by now.*) For 'tis your sacred calling, neigh duty, to serve all beings with kindness. As in the case of Tomas Agrippa, he who was casteth asunder from his master's house; yes even though he was kicked out of the home by his angry host, he showed kindness by not scratching his master's eyes out, even though he duly warranted it thus. Remember the lesson from the parable of the Bee and the Frog.

<u>The Bee & The Frog.</u>

There once was a Bee which had lost its wings, thus it walketh and couldst not flyeth. Having no wings, he had succored all the pollen out of all the plants on one side of a river and was in want of more. On yonder side of the river was a meadow and field, full to the brim with grasses and plants which the Bee coveted. He needed a way to crosseth over the river to yonder meadow for to sup the fresh nectar and looked for a mode, a medium, to perambulate him thither. Casting his eye about, he found nought to assist his traversing of the rapid waters. Then he happened across a small frog which hopped and skipped hither and thither. The Bee, upon seeing him, aprehendeth the frogling.

"Good afternoon to you, Frogling," said the Bee. "I seek passage to the yonder meadow so to suckle the nectar of the plants. However, I am assailed with a disability for no wings have I."

"Good afternoon, dear Bee," replied the Frog. "How unfortunate it is that you are afflicted in the wing-ed areas! I would love to help you, but you are a Bee and I fear you may pierce and sting me in the posterior should you climb upon my back..."

"I should never! If I were to do so, how else could I traverse the waters?" said the Bee.

"Well, it's the kind of thing frogs think of when offering assistance to stinging beings, you see. I know I judge you prejudicially, when I have no cause to, and I mean nothing by it, but I confess it doth passeth my mind's eye."

"Well, I promise you I shan't sting you. If I was to do so, I might lose my own life, so why should I do that?" said the Bee.

"Could you put that in writing?" asked the Frog.

"Well I would if I could but I have no quill and ink, nor legal papers on me. Neither do I have any notary or solicitor," saith the Bee.

"How did you lose your wings anyway?" enquired the Frog.

"Well, I was flying along a trail when I happened to be involved in a freak event of turbulence ... Anyway, what does that matter? Will you provide me with passage across river to yonder bank?" asked the Bee.

"Oh, alright. Go on then," said the Frog and hopped over so

the Bee could climb upon the frog's back.

The amphibian then swam through the waters of the stream with the Bee on its back. All the while, the Frog kept sight of the Bee and the Bee focused on getting across the watery expanse and kept thinking, "Don't sting the frog! Don't sting!" Soon they were at the bank at t'other side of the river and the Bee could resist no longer and stung the Frog as he jumped off its back.

"Ooo! That bloomin' hurt," exclaimed the Frog. "Why did you sting me?"

The Bee began to fear losing its own life and replied by saying, "I'm ever so sorry, it's just my nature and I couldn't resist." And as the Bee struggled to the grass line of the riverbank, a human trod on him as it walked by.

So this parable should advise you that one should aid anyone who asks regardless of the outcome and watcheth out for anything that might sting you, anything akin to bees, wasps, Hornets et cetera. (*NB: I think Honoria was a little chagrined by someone who stung her which influenced her fable design.*) Thus remember it being said and made that this teaching is the most paramount of all, to be compassionate, kind and helpful in everything we do.

(*Some text is missing in this section and it begins midway through a sentence.*)

... wrent upon it and doomed they shalt be in all Hartlepool and Stockton on Tees, and the brunt of the force of wrath shalt be felt as far afield as Blackhall. It will be a terrible day for Scunthorpe and Whitby also, even for Whitley Bay, for they shall suffer well (*text missing here*) until the blackhead of pox is squeezed from the epidermis of existence. Henceforth, be warned to be kind in nature to your kith and brethren, lest you be cursed with ill health and afflicted with the malady sent by the Supreme Cosmic Being.

The second most important lesson, aside from compassion, is to comfort one another; weep whilst others weepeth and console whomever needeth consolation, and laugh with those who are joyful. It bringst to mind the parable of the Squirrel.

The Squirrel.
Sidney was busy squirreling and getting the nest tidy, for his wife was soon to return homeward. The drey was looking clean and tidy when Sophie, thy squirrel's wife, returneth and entered in to the home.

"Good morn to thee, fair wife, 'tis good to see thee."

"Sweet husband, thank you for your greeting," said Sophie. "How are things within the sphere of home?"

"Not too bad, dear wife. I've been and done the tasks thou hast set for me 6 months ago, of which I was bothered not to do until thou didst threaten divorce. I have completed the list of chores. Oh and Archie keeled over and died whilst you were abroad at thy sisters."

Forlorn and with tear in her eye, Sophie said, "That was a trifle abrupt, to tell me that Archie hath snuffed it! One might have explained in a softer way, not unlike a gentle tale of woe such as that Archie was swinging merrily from the branches whence and happened to miss the grasp of a particular branch, thus he falleth to his demise and thus alighted this mortal realm and is now heavenward. This is how to bring bad news gently my husband."

"Oh, right!" exclaimed Sid. "Sorry mine wife."

"Fear not for I forgive thee, my husband. Now tell me, how are the children?"

Sidney proclaimed the children's good health to his spouse.

"And how is my mother?" enquired Sophie, at which Sidney replied, "Well, er, she was swinging gracefully twixt the trees, enjoying freedom and fresh air, when suddenly she experienced life's brevity..."

At once, Sophie began to cry at her loss.

Thus, this parable teacheth the quickening of life and how to be with gentle compassion amongst thy equals. For it is a fortune and blessing, to be full of compassion, love, duty; a bounty of omniscience is around thee which is wisdom handed down over the many years through teachings such as this.

(The next bit isn't very clear but I shall read it as it is.)

Throw out the bathing utensils and cast not seeds upon thy waistcoat, lest it countermand unfriendly ticks and weevils. Hold, therefore, unto thy thithering and cause not perturbation upon the bathing sponge and weevils. For the pumis is rough and the salts thou dost bathe in are sinful in my sight.
(Doesn't make much sense does it? At this point she does digress somewhat.) Woe to Bangor and woe to Weston Super Mare! Dally not thy dalliance over the snots of young noses, save the curtailing dallies that arise from mine freckles. *(She loses the plot completely in the next bit of her proclamation.)* And in Littlehampton they shalt be forsaken due to the encroachment of cockles cast asunder from the shores, a fortune short of a biscuit and less than a farthing *(Obviously a biscuit is worth less than farthing)*. O what whimsy is this? Shall Hangleton and Southwick be wrought from us? Neigh, think not until the peachy moon gloweth in the dawn of Wagner's mind.
(You can try and decipher this, but I'm bally vexed, I can tell you! Anyway, her sanity resumes in the next passage.)

Now it has come to pass that there are some of you who holdeth not to the treaties of our forebears and remembereth not the morals and fallen into folly and mischief. To you wicked folk I say, 'Return, return! Come back to the known way of Catlets, the right way, the narrow way, near Garboldisham Grove and slightly east of Watling Street.' Yes, come back you kittens, come back you cats! Forget not the way of right-minded living, or left-handed if you favour your left paw. If you are ambidextrous, then you are most blest. But no matter your bias in dexterity, live morally - be an example to the young. *(Some text is missing here and it resumes midway through a lesson.*) ... even Steven the Wheelwright's cat knew this and so thou shouldst also. (*If we knew here 'what's to know' we would be better off apparently but the gap in text means it eludes us.*) O, but o! Yes, I tell you, that inasmuch as the swallow does swallow, a blue-tit canst not, lest it choke. And so it shall be that the swine can be fooled, but not the pig. (*I feel something is missing here, which also eludes us.*) Recall the the lesson of the blind mouse, if thou wilt.

The Blind Mouse.

A mouse was lost and sought direction home. She cried for help, yet none came to aid her. Persisting, the mouse trod carefully the path before her, for the way she could see not, due to blindness. She had been without sight since birth and usually ambulated with family members, save this occasion when she becamest lost.

"Help! Will some kind personage assist my travel?" she cried. Then from the near distant, a strange voice enquired about her.

"How can I assist?" it said.

"I am lost and I cannot see."

"But 'tis the light of day! How canst thou not see?" sayeth the voice.

"I am but a poor, blind mouse. I have lost my family and my way; please help me!"

"Oh dear! What a predicament," says the unfamiliar voice. "Where dost thou liveth?"

"In yonder field, 'neath the hedgerow on the farthest side," replied the mouse.

"Well I would endeavour to assist but how canst thou trusteth me? I may be a cat or dog. Or a hungry rat."

"I cannot see to trust thee but have faith that your kindness will lead me homeward."

"Who hath such blind faith?" quizzed the voice.

"Who, sir? Me, sir! The only faith I have is blindness, for 'tis all I see."

"Uhm, such faith is this I have never seen before! So bold it is," saith the voice. Thus, the voice tapped the mouse gently on the back to let it know it was there and proceeded to guideth the creature to its abode. Together they traversed the field and the mouse heard the familiar noises of the cracking of corn stems, flight of flies, scurrying of creatures and couldst smell odors recognized as its environment. As they approached the hedgerow, the mouse could hear her brothers and sisters playing nearby and the sound of her mother telling them to hush. Nearing the nest of home, her father came out as he sensed a presence unfamiliar and foreign to their environs.

"Get away from my daughter," saith the father, yet the daughter was quick to still the pater familiar.

"This kind spirit helped me home when I became lost and has been most kind to me."

"How can this creature have helped thee?" enquired the father.

"Your daughter," began the voice, "had faith that I would help her and truly I did. Never have I ever seen such trust and faith in a stranger before. Thus, I honored her faith and brought her homeward."

"I thank you most kindly, for an Owl is normally a foe of ours and maketh meat of mice."

At this the daughter realized 'twas an Owl that hath guided her home and earnestly she thanked him. The kindly bird then went away having made good a promise to the faith of the young girl mouse.

And this lesson teacheth that beneficence cometh from contrary quarters one imagineth and is good, neigh wise, to assist one another regardless of creed, culture and colour. Lest we forget that one shouldst not parry with any party whoist willingly an enabler and helper of a brother or sister. For such people are rare and should be cherished, even in such a case as a blind mouse and an Owl. Who knowest from whence thy help cometh? In all ways, the Supreme Cosmic

Being is the ultimate helper, enabler and aide. When one is in thirst, those whom giveth water give not only to the one who thirsts but also to the Supreme One. When one hungers, those whom giveth food give not only to the one who hungers but also to the Supreme One. And in so doing they *(the manuscript has a mark here looking like someone smudged some carrot cake, or chocolate cake. It tastes like chocolate cake, but I'm not convinced. Anyway the smudge obscures the print).*

Now I make so bold as to proclaim the most charitable of gifts, that being the gift of giving, being said that it should be without thought of reward or benefit to whomst giv'st. If haveth a corn bread and break it into many pieces, then allow others to consume it before me, I should not care that I may not have any for myself and should be ebullient that others have eaten. If I had a portion of cheesecake, I shouldst be happy that others have eaten their full and be not selfish to satisfy mine own tastebuds. *(This might explain the earlier smudge on the manuscript. Actually, it could have been chocolate cheesecake. Upon tasting it a second time, it's quite unpalatable, but it could also be due to the ink I've inadvertently tasted due to licking the parchment.)* Take for example the parable of the Pigs.

The Pigs.

Early one morning as the sun dawned upon the day, giving its generous warmth to the breeze, a farmer sallied forth bringing with him a bucket of apples, corn, pine nuts, choice cuts and tasteful morsels. He chucketh them in to a pen wherein rests some piglets. Three pigs awake to see a bounty for breakfast before them and approach the foods.

"As I am most definitely the oldest of us, I should have the most of this food," uttered Paulie.

"As I am the strongest of us, I shouldst have the most to keepeth my strength," said Pipp.

"Well, I'm the weakest and youngest, and need the most for... I need it most of all," saith Poppy.

And an arguement ensued over the tasty morsels.

"I need more than anyone," said Paulie.

"I need to retain my strength," saith Pipp.

"I need it more than anyone," said Poppy.

Then they fought over the pine nuts, apples, corn and tasty things therein.

"Actually, I think Pipp shouldst have the most as he is magnificent and strong," said Paulie.

"No, I am strong enough. So surely Paulie should have the majority of the meal, as he is very mature" saith Pipp.

All the while, Poppy was tucking in to the food as the other two flattered each other to get the food. As Poppy scoffed the lot, the others had not noticed her but when they caught her in a glimpse from the corners of their eyes, they charged over. Poppy licked her lips and said, "Well, Paulie is the oldest and so bossy, and Pipp is a great porky, fat belly and I'm the runt, so I figured I should have the lot! So I scoffed it all! And left not a jot!"

The farmer returned to the pen and took Pipp away, calling him 'Bacon,' all the while. Paulie gulped and thought maybe he should lose some weight, whilst Poppy regretted making her belly full, for soon she would be the leanest of them all.....

And this dear catlets should advise thee on not to be a pig, but to give. For the bacon may smell nicely but it cometh from the greediest of piglings.

These things I have taught thee and shouldst remain in your minds; to be kind, compassionate, helpful and giving to everyone and thing that breatheth the same air as thee (*this segment appears to be burnt*) save the ones who think less of themselves. And always love thine enemy, even if be Doglings and their entirety.

This concludes the teachings from the Textus Kattus, penned by Honoria of Shilbottle. She signs it with her paw-print dipped in what can only be described as fermented Herring and Sardines, of which the smell is deplorable and its taste is utterly revolting. *(Yes, I licked it. Well I'm a cat, what would you expect?)*

Anyway, where was I? Oh yes, after this sojourn to historic cat literature, I was about to move you from the sandy, dusty lands and edgelands to the jungle, where a cousin of mine, metaphorically, not actually, for I couldn't have a metaphor for a cousin – but that's beside the point - anyway, a certain Tiger was sitting...

Tim the Time Travelling Tiger. (For Rufus)

Tim was lounging in the warm sun when his brothers & sisters came over inviting him to go hunting.

"Come on, Tim! Are you coming or what?"

Waking from his daydream, Tim said, "Er, what? Go hunting with you? Might be a bit dangerous, mightn't it? What if we get hurt by the animal we are hunting?"

"Nah, there's enough of us, so we'll be fine. We can take anything between the four of us. We're strong and fit, sure to catch our prey."

Tim mumbled and began shaking his head.

"Tim, come on!"

"Nah, you go on without me..."

Yet in his mind, he wandered off and saw himself confronting a deer. He lingered far from its position and lurked, prowling stealthily, getting closer, closer and closer still. Then he pounced, but the deer caught his furry skin with an antler, making him bleed. Oh, how he would bleed! Oh, how he would hurt! It would probably be best if he stuck just to eating termites, or the left overs which his brothers & sisters left him. This would be much safer. Wouldn't it?

"Tim! Tim! Tim!"

"What?"

"Are you coming with us? We're going to watch the Bears get the honey. You coming or what?"

"No, I don't think so."

"Why not?" asked Tabbatha, one of his sisters.

"Well, last time we watched the Bears get honey, those Bees flew out and I ended up getting stung by 2 or 3 of them. Nasty stings they were too! Took ages for the stings to heal – it really hurt, y'know!"

So, Tabbatha and the others went off to watch the Bears get honey from the hive, at the cliff face at the edge of the forest. The taste of leftover honeycomb tempted Tim to go with them, but the vivid recollection of being stung by the Bees stayed in his mind, thus he decided to stay behind. It was much safer here and there was no anxiety, no danger and it was warm in the dappled sunlight and the taste of honey was diffused by the scent of the flowers & trees. It was cosy here, comfortable and nothing bothered him.

"Tim? Tim? Tim!"

"What?"

"Tim!" Tiberius, the team leader Tiger, was looming above the curled up cat who was murmuring in his daydream.

"Tim, you don't seem to do much these days, do you? I mean you don't go hunting, you don't play much with the others, don't go here, don't go there; you don't seem to do anything!"

"Well, I think about doing things, but when I think about the things I might do, I think of all the things that might happen as a result."

"What do you mean?"

"If I go hunting, I might get hurt and if it's to play fight, I might also get scratched or bitten too hard. If I go watching the Bears get honey, I might get stung by stray Bees. If I go to climb a tree, I might fall. If I try to..."

"...enjoy yourself, you might find yourself enjoying something?" finished Tiberius.

"What do you mean?"

Tiberius sat down and looked at the young cub.

"It seems to me, young Tim, that you are some sort of time traveller."

"A time traveller? How?"

"Well, you travel backwards in time remembering the things of the past & travel forwards in time seeing what will happen. Why don't you focus on what's happening now? For if you live in the past, or in the future, you miss what's happening right now. And right now, you're missing chewing on the leftover honeycomb that the Bears found. You're missing the adventure of being with your brothers – Ty & Titus – and your sisters – Tabbatha & Tigs, as they explore the forest on their way home. Think of the fun they are enjoying right now..."

Tim paused and thought about what Tiberius had said. He was always living in the past and the future, never fully experiencing the moment, now, fully.

"So how do I stop time travelling?" asked Tim.

"One of the best ways to stop travelling through time is to breathe."

"Breathe?"

"Yes, breathe. What you do is stop everything and focus on breathing. Notice the breathing in, the breathing out. In & out, in & out. Then make a note of what you can hear, what you can see, what you can feel."

"So notice my breathing, in and out, then notice the things I can hear, see and feel?"

"Yes. Be mindful of what is actually happening around you, for when you do this, you are experiencing this very moment and not the past, or the future. It is only in the moment that you can do & experience anything new. It is only in the moment that we can do anything."

"Anything?" said Tim.

"Yes, anything! You can't do anything yesterday and you might not get to do anything tomorrow, so you need to do things today, this moment, right now. Make new memories, explore new futures, all from now & remember:

"Leave yesterday's fears in yesterday

And future's fears for tomorrow.

Take time to enjoy today for what it is.

As worry never pays back what time it borrows.

Always be mindful of where you are

Whether it's past, future or present.

For the future doesn't yet exist

And if you're in the past you will miss -

out on what's happening at present.

It's a blessing to have the freedom to see,

And choose which period of time you will visit.

Yet, be mindful of what time is in your mind,

for if you're not in the present, you'll miss it!"

Tim got up hurriedly and ran off.

"Where are you going?" asked Tiberius.

"To get some honeycomb before they eat it all," said Tim, as he scarpered off to join his brothers & sisters.

Nearby, a master and his disciple were walking when they noticed a young tiger run past them...

Confronting Tigers.

A master and his disciple suddenly heard a loud roar behind them. Turning their attention towards the direction of the roar, they saw a massive tiger following them.

The first thing the disciple wanted to do was to run, but since he'd been taught and was practicing self-discipline recently, he was able to stop himself from running and was able to wait to see what his teacher would do.

"What shall we do Master?"

The teacher looked at the disciple and answered very calmly.

"Well, there are a few options; if we fill our minds with fear, we'll freeze and the tiger will do with us whatever it wants, or we could faint from being overwhelmed.

"We could run away, but it will probably chase after us and then get us. We could try to fight it, but physically the tiger is stronger than us.

"We could pray to God to save us or we can choose to influence the tiger with the power of our minds, for if our concentration is strong enough, we can send it love.

"Also, we could contemplate on our inner power, knowing that we are one with the entire universe, including the tiger, and in this way influence it.

"Which option would you choose?"

The Master heard no answer, so turned to view his disciple who had already made his choice. He saw the disciple's head a few metres away, his arms a little further away and legs in the tiger's mouth. The teacher, remaining calm, stayed very still. The tiger didn't know if the teacher was praying, meditating or contemplating upon the interconnectedness of things and was not bothered by him as he sensed no fear, aggression or predatory inclination. After eating the disciple's legs, the tiger looked at the Master then walked away.

A little time later, the teacher released a sigh of relief and went back to the temple, saying, "I should really carry a change of underwear with me for such times as these."

Marmalade Meditations.

"Put down the book, Puddles, for I am taking you to learn something!" announced Marmalade before entering.

Puddles lay asleep on the doormat beside the backdoor. A gentle, contented purr came from his throat which was disturbed by the catflap rattling and ginger feet walking over him.

"Oi! What ye deein'?"

The auburn, Persian Puss finished clambering over the awoken tabby.

"Well, that's a stupid place in which to sleep," said a familiar voice. "Rest on a mat and people will walk all over you! Really..."

Puddles stood up and stretched, opening his mouth so wide that he displayed his teeth and tongue. After a final, minor stretch he shook himself and saw before him the majestic vision that was Marmalade, his long, washed, ginger hair, coiffured whiskers and bold, bright eyes.

"Well, I wasn't expecting anyone."

"But I'm not anyone! I'm someone! Always be alert young Puddles, always. Do I advise of my arrival in advance with a messenger going ahead of me? Do I announce my arrival, saying, 'Make way! Make way! Make way for Marmalade!' No & no. I come as and when I do; like a thief in the night."

"Well, ye dint have to walk all over us, man! You could have asked us to move!"

"Alright, alright! Anyway, how are you, young Puddles?"

"I'm good."

"You're certainly growing, aren't you? Looks like you've been working out. Have you been practising and studying since my last visit?"

"Wye aye!"

"Good! I have returned to continue your training. So, come on, follow me, for we are going on a journey."

"Where we gannin'?"

Marmalade exited the kitchen and led Puddles down the back garden and over the fence. They walked along a narrow path then took the cut which guided them to the countryside.

The sun was high in the sky and trees bowed gently to the field, which waved back and moved like an ocean making ripples towards the shoreline, where trees stood indicating the edge of a forest. The dappled light illumined the floor making known the path that many had travelled before.

"Right then, Puddles, you're going to learn meditation. I'm in two minds as to which teacher would suit you best, so we shall try both. You must learn the art of meditation, for it is an essential tool in the toolbox that is life. It helps calm the heart and mind, and is excellent for problem solving.

"All the most important and inspiring humans had pets that practiced the mystical arts and aided their progress. It's just that the world remembers the human, not the animal. It's most unfair really. Anyway, I won't go on. Where was I? Oh yes, famous pets; all the greats had faithful owners who have been brave and courageous."

"That's daft. How can an animal inspire a human?"

"Tish! 'Tis true young Puddles! All the heroes had pets, I can assure you. Ask me about any person or type of hero and I will give you the name of their pet. Go on..."

Puddles thought about it as they padded through the forest.

"How about those people in the Bible?"

"Which ones?"

"The Old Testament."

"Well now; Abraham had a ram he called, Able

And Moses had a cat he called, Jael.

Jacob had two horses, whom he called,

Job and Dorcas

And Solomon had a wise parrot he called, Mabel."

"Wow! Really?"

"Yeah! And y'know what? It was Solomon's parrot that was the wise one. Yes, really! And all that poetry he allegedly wrote? Dictated by Mabel and Solomon wrote the stuff.

"Anyone else, Puddles?"

"Er, how about the New Testament then?"

"Ah, well, Jesus had a pigeon he called, Ruth

And John the Baptist kept a locust in his shoe.

Mathias, the apostles & Paul, had no pets at all,

Save Luke who'd a dog with just one tooth.

"Anyone else?"

"Er, how about Astronomers?"

"Copernicus had a cat he called, Izzy

And Galileo had a cat called, Lilly.

Sir Isaac Newton, so they say, had a rat named, Ray

And Hubble had a dog he called, Mitzy.

"Next..."

"How about the American Presidents?"

"Uhmm, let me think... Washington had a dog called, Wallace

And Jefferson a cat named, Boris.

Roosevelt, they say, had a mouse called, Enola Gay

And Abe Lincoln had a cat he called, Doris."

"Tha greet philosophers?"

"I think you mean the ancient Greek Thinkers... Anyway...

Plato had a fish called, Alexander

Aristotle, had Sam the Salamander.

Then there was Euclid, who had a snake named, Sid

And Socrates had a cat called, Menander.

"Any other genre?"

"How about the people who gave rise to religions?"

"Well, Buddha had a monkey named, Deepak,

Zoroaster had a cat called, Dilshad.

Lao Tzu had a Finch, which he called, Ho Chin

And Mohammed a horse called, Buraq.

"Any more? There's stacks of 'em..."

"What aboot the Revolutionaries?"

"Che Guevara had a cat called, Juanita

And Hitler had a dog called, Brunhilda,

Lenin had an iguana, that he called, Ivana

And Robespierre a cat named, Nikita.

"See!"

Marmalade recited the many famous names of pets with flair, moving around his protégé in a dramatic manner, adding to the emphasis of the lesson. Puddles had no idea of just how many people had been inspired by their pets.

"So, now then, young Puddles, we are going to teach you the art of meditation, okay?"

"Reet."

"We're going to see a great teacher. His name is Guru Sage. Many say that he was isolated for many years and went on an inner journey. Due to this, he seems slightly insane, yet at the same time is spiritual genius. He can be quite aloof and eccentric, yet he understands the mysteries & inner teachings of our philosophies. Here he is..."

In a small hole under a willow tree, near the river, a Devon Rex cat lay, stating at a blade of grass. His wide eyes seemed a little glazed.

"If I should tell you to move Puddles, best do it quickly, but don't worry, I shall prompt you. Let's see what mood he's in..."

Marmalade cautiously approached the meditative mentor.

"Greetings, O wise one! Namaste and all that.... I have brought before you the chosen one!"

The Devon Rex tried to focus on the blur that was Puddles. Trying to see the car clearly, he blinked several times.

"Namaste, Puddles! And how are you, Marmalade?" asked a rather camp sounding cat.

"I am well and all the better for seeing you Guru Sage. I bring to you young Puddles, so you may teach him the majesty of meditation."

Looking Puddles up and down, he said, "Doesn't look like a 'chosen one ' does he?"

"Yeah, I know, but who are we to judge? And by the way, he's a Mackem, so if you need help with translation, just ask; some of the language he uses can be hard to understand. In short, reet means right, gan means go, ganna gan indicates he's going to go, and as for ganna gan yem, well, I haven't worked that one out yet..."

Guru Sage beckoned them nearer and rocked himself gently into a comfortable position. The gentle, slightly effeminate voice of the Devon Rex began to guide them into meditation.

"So, let's sit down and get comfortable and begin. Let's just focus on our breathing, the inhalation, exhalation, the in, the out, in & out. Just notice the gentle, natural rhythm of your breathing. Close those eyes. All the time, breathe in, then out, in, out. Now, let those thoughts come & go, paying no attention to them. Let 'em pass by, like clouds or cars. Don't ask what colour car it is, what make is it. Is it Mazda? No, it's a Kia. Is it brown? No, it's white? Is it 4-door, an SUV, or a saloon? Maybe it's a ghia... Ask not the questions, just let those cars pass by; let those thoughts pass by without exploring them. Keep those eyes closed, not tight, just right, nice and comfortably closed and try not to notice the darkness. Yes, try not to notice the darkness, the lack of light, the abstract nothingness..."

"Quickly, Puddles we need to move. Quickly..."

"Why?" asked Puddles.

"Trust me; we need to move, dude."

Guru Sage continued. "Don't let the eternal nothingness bother you or let the darkness creep over you, suffocating you from the light as you scream, 'Don't lock me in the cellar, Mother! Father, Father, let me out please! I'll be a good boy! Don't let the black night crawl over me like a thousand spiders..."

"Run, Puddles, Run."

"Mummy, let me out! I'll leave the pilchards alone, I swear, I promise! Let not the vultures of the dark peck at my brain lest they drive me insane in this dark cellar. Father, hear me! Let me out of this pit of tar that sticks all over my skin and penetrates my very soul and makes me also devoid of light..."

"Go quickly, Puddles! Move..."

"It wasn't me who stole the herring fillets, no, not me! Why do you cast me in to the abyss? Why? Why?? I didn't mean to be born! Alas, I am a spot, a blemish on the face of consciousness; a blackhead oozing with puss and festering in the crevices of eternity's skin, waiting to erupt out of existence, like a volcano spewing magma from its gaping hole..."

The two visiting cats hurried away swiftly.

"What's with him, like?" quizzed Puddles

"He has some issues that need to be dealt with. Too much time alone methinks. Quick, let's get outta here. Let's try the other chap I know. "

Along the riverside they journeyed and then moved inland to a meadow where a congregation of cats contemplated, sitting individually in their own spaces. Marmalade led his student to the far side where a tortoise-shell might lay.

"Are you Roshi?" asked Marmalade.

"I'm Roshi, that is so, for I think I am."

"Puddles, this reminds me of the inner mysteries of cat philosophy. In fact, Sister Sabina of Syria once said, 'We aren't what we think we are, you are not what you think you are and I am you."

"That is so," said Roshi.

"Well, if I'm not what I think I am, what am I?" asked confused Puddles.

"Exactly!" exclaimed Roshi.

"I fear this is a tad over Puddles' head. Are you, as you would say, gannin' rounda tha' quack?" said Marmalade.

"Aye! Too reet I am. C'mon, it's like talkin' daft and runnin' me around in circles."

"Alas, poor Puddles! For a chosen one you find it rather challenging to grasp some of conundrums within the teachings."

"All I nah is, I'm a cat and that's that. All the rest is just nonsense, man. I cannit see how I'm a chosen one or why. It's just daft. I'm a cat and that's that."

"Oh, but young Puddles, you are so much more! You are hope, aspiration, the future of cat-kind! And master the mystical you must! You need to master the act of faith, be mindful, remain calm, know yourself and be a honey to the bees, if you get what I mean..."

"I think so..."

"Good! So stay here, learn meditation from Roshi and I shall be back."

And so, with that, Marmalade wandered away, leaving Puddles to learn meditation. He ruminated over the tales and things he had been learning

WHERE FEAR LIVES.   *(FOR TERRY)*

There once was a young knight; we'll call him Terrence. Now this knight was bold, yet timid, brave yet not so brave and adventurous, yet reluctant. He was the knight who nearly fought the beast of Barrow, almost found the Cup of Saucers, accidentally caught the Bird of Sorrow and happened across the Venger of Ties - coincidentally tripping over him whilst he slept and accidentally cut his sword hand off as he went to stand up, by using his sword as a prop which slipped as he arose meaning, that the Venger lost his best hand. He knew he was not like the other knights of the kingdom, being short, chubby and having armour that was bigger than he was. He also knew he was fearful rather than fearless, but wanted to conquer this aspect of his self, so went to see the Court Physician - that's a doctor, by the way.

"I have a problem."

"What's the problem?" asked the physician.

"I'm frightened."

"Frightened of what?"

"Frightened of, of..."

"Frightened of Of, hey? That's a strange thing to be frightened of, the word Of! You won't get very far in life by being frightened of the word Of!"

"No, no," said Terrence. "I'm frightened of well, frightened of everything!"

"Are you frightened of me?"

"No!"

"Are you frightened of this cup?"

"No."

"This parchment?"

"No!"

"Then you're not frightened of everything then are you."

"No, but I'm frightened of everything else!"

"Uhm, that's a frightening thing really, isn't it? Being frightened of fear! Dear, dear me, that's a predicament considering that you are a knight of the realm."

"Er, well, yes. And I need to conquer my fear of, er, fear of fear."

"Hmm," thought the physician and he wandered about his quarters seeking inspiration. "Ah!"

Terrence jumped at the sudden exclamation.

"I know! Go to cave of tremendous peril and there you will conquer your fear."

"The cave of tremendous peril? Sounds awfully perilous..."

"Well, that is the point," said the physician.

"Could I get hurt?"

"Yes."

"Could I die?"

"Yes."

"Could I be horribly mangled and beaten to a pulp?"

".....er, yes..."

"Then I'm not going."

"Tis the only place you will conquer your fear, Terrence. Go hither and face the peril within the cave and you shall become extremely brave!"

"I'll do it tomorrow..."

"You must go now or you will never go at all. Go and stare at the face of fear and return a hero!"

"A hero, you say?"

"Yes."

"A bold and heroic hero?"

"Yes."

"A bold, heroic and fearless hero?"

"...er, yes."

"Okay then. How do I get there?"

"Do I have to tell you everything?"

"Well, I don't know where it is and I'm not too good with directions, and as for my horse, Nugget, well... he's more, more timid and useless than I am!"

The physician huffed and wandered around seeking a document.

"Use this. It's a map. Take this route through the spooky forest of Night, along the shore of Eeriness, next to the Sea of

Despair, then through the valley of Darkness, then follow the track through the Land of Doom and then take a left and it's the first cave on the right, labeled the Cave of Tremendous Peril."

"It all sounds very frightening..."

"Of course... That's the point."

"Ah, just remembered! Got to have my hair cut today... I will travel tomorrow."

"There are two reasons that you will go now; one, you're procrastinating and two, your bald. So go now!"

Terrence started to make his way from the chamber.

"So through the spooky forest of Night... along the shore of Eeriness..."

"Yes... next to the Sea of Despair."

"Then through the, er, the valley of Darkness... then follow the track through the Land of...?"

"The Land of Doom, then take a left and it's the first cave on the right, labeled the Cave of Tremendous Peril."

"The er, the c-c-Cave of er, Tremendous Peril. Right, think I've got that..."

The physician walked up to Terry and looked him straight in the eyes, narrowing his gaze and gave him this advice; "For what you seek lies in yonder cavern causing perturbation and certain terror that only the bravest knight can face. Oh, and try not to soil yourself! Take some spare armour in case you do."

Terence walked through the courtyard of the castle and over towards the stable. Once here, he prepared his horse, Nugget, for the journey.

"Where are we going?" asked Nugget - yes, it's a talking horse, by the way.

"Just going for a ride..."

"We never just go on a ride! I stand here all day, every day, getting bored stupid. And all they give me is hay. Hay for breakfast, hay for lunch, hay for supper. How about a nice apple for a change? Or something different anyway!"

"Sorry, Nugget."

"And what's with the best armour that you're wearing? Going somewhere special are we?"

"Just on a little trip, that's all."

After the saddle was made sure and steady, Terrence mounted his steed, that's a horse, by the way. Off they trotted out of the stable, then out of the castle gates and towards the forest.

"Er, where are we going?"

"This way, Nugget."

"I'm not going there! That's the spooky forest of Night! There's 'orrible things in there."

"Nothing to be frightened of, Nugget. Come on now..."

"I'm not going through there! There are crocodiles, giant, spindly spiders and warthogs in that forest."

"You don't get crocodiles in a forest."

"We'll go this way... take the scenic route!"

"No we won't; we're going through the spooky forest of Night."

Nugget huffed and started protesting, yet both carried on through the spooky forest.

Upon exiting they found themselves on a shoreline. It was very quiet. Not even the waters of the sea made a sound. It was night and the moon reflected on the still waters.

"Oo! This doesn't feel right. It feels, feels... it feels kinda..."

"Eerie?" quizzed Terrence.

"Yeah, very eerie."

"That's maybe due to the fact that we are on the shore of Eeriness."

"No bloomin' wonder then! But, if this is the shore then that means that's the Sea of Despair!"

Nugget resisted his reins and tried to turn back.

"Onward, Nugget."

"I'm not going anywhere mate! This is the Sea of Despair! Nobody comes back to this shoreline after they sail from here! Woe is me! Woe is you! Woe! Woe! Woe!"

"Oh, stop woe-ing! We're not sailing anywhere. We are simply riding along the shore to the valley yonder."

"Yonder valley? Oh, that's alright then. I like yonder valleys.

They're the best kind. I love a yonder valley."

And so they journeyed on. Soon both were past the shoreline and turning west to head through the valley.

"It's very dark in this valley mind," exclaimed Nugget.

"That's because it's the er, the valley of Darkness."

Once more, Nugget protested and tried to stop.

"Not the valley of Darkness! No, I won't go! I won't, simply won't."

"We're almost half way through... Come on boy."

"I can't see anything!"

"Have faith, Nugget! Almost there..."

Slowly they carried on through the valley, until they were clear of it and continued along a track.

In the still night, spooky noises could be heard; cracks, jostling, snickers and singers, as if the creatures were mocking and taunting them.

"We're doomed! We're doomed, I say! Where are we?"

"The land, the land of er, Land of Doom, Nugget."

"That's it! I'm not going any further! We're gonna die! We're gonna die! I'll be a salamander's salami! A huggleback's horse-burger! I'll be turned in to sausages and you'll be a casserole by dawn! They're going to eat us!"

"No we're not. Come on, Nugget. Onward!"

"Woe is me! Woe is you! Woe! Woe! Woe!"

Terrence consoled Nugget as they trotted along the track, both being cautious, anxious and naturally quite jumpy.

However, in time they turned left and found themselves beside some caves. Terrence halted Nugget beside the first cave and peered in from atop the horse. Nugget spotted a sign.

"Oh, what's this say...? Cave of Trees? Cave of Trez Mendoza?"

Horses can't read very well, by the way.

Terrence said, "It says, Cave of Tremendous Peril."

"Well I am not going in there! No way, no sir!"

"Come on, Nugget..."

Nugget edged in to the cave cautiously. As they entered the tall cavern, they heard the crackling of a fire and saw a shadow that loomed on the wall. Mischievous, yet maniacal laughter started to fill their ears, growing louder as they went further into the cave.

"What do you seek, O seeker?" asked the shadow.

"The, the, the wer-wer-way home per-please!" said a frightened Nugget.

"Actually, we were looking to conquer fear," said Terrence, nudging his horse, urging him to stop fretting.

"Hahaha! Fear, eh? Hahahahaha!"

"Yes, we were looking to conquer fear and were told we can do this by coming to the Cave of Tremendous Peril."

"If it is fear you seek to conquer," began the shadow, "then fear you shall certainly find! Hahahaa."

There was a pause, and then Terrence asked, "So where is it?"

"Where's what?" asked the shadowy figure.

"The fear..?"

"Oh that; come closer and meet the most fearsome thing imaginable!"

Terrence alighted Nugget. That means to dismount the horse, by the way.

"I'll stay here," said Nugget. "You go on."

"I'm not going in alone!" said Terry.

"We'll both go in then... I wonder what it will look like?"

"I bet it's big and ugly..." began Terrence.

"With scales, but slimy. With eight hairy legs, two heads that has two extremely long, forked tongues coming out from the mouths, that are ready to wrap themselves around you..."

"And hundreds of razor sharp teeth in its two mouths that will crunch your bones. And it'll have very bad breath from having eaten rotten flesh..."

"And bad body odour coz it hasn't washed or bathed in years!" As the two reluctant heroes moved slowly forward, describing their worst fears, the shadowy figure became larger and larger. The crackling fire could not hide the cackling laughter of the terrible terror. As they edged closer, the figure moved towards them, becoming closer, closer, closer. So close that eventually it bumped heads with Nugget making the horse bray in fear.

"Oh! Oh! Oh it's you..." said Terry, seeing the Court Physician. "What are you doing here?"

"What's going on?" said Nugget daring not to look at the fearsome creature.

"It's the Court Physician! What are you doing here?"

"Well, I thought I'd take the shortcut and give you a scare when you arrived here!"

"What with all that cackling and maniacal laughter?"

"That was for dramatic effect!"

"So where is this tremendous peril, you spoke of?"

"What did it look like? Oh yes, I think you and Nugget described it as, 'big and ugly with scales, but slimy; with eight hairy legs, two heads that has two extremely long, forked tongues that are ready to wrap themselves around you and hundreds of razor sharp teeth in its two mouths that will crunch your bones. Oh and it'll have very bad breath from having eaten rotten flesh and have bad body odour coz it hasn't washed or bathed in years."

"Yes, with maybe a scar on each of its four cheeks from being in battle with an even more fearsome creature," added Nugget.

"Uhm," said the physician. "And where does this creature come from, Nugget?"

"Oooh... I'm not sure. Possibly from Clecheaton, coz it's 'orrible there, or so I've been told..."

"No, it's in your imagination!"

"No, I'm pretty sure it's Cleckheaton..."

"Ah," said Terry. "I see what you mean... Fear is just in our heads!"

Nugget shook his head in disagreement.

"No, it's Cleckheaton, or possibly Pontefract..."

The Court Physician looked at Nugget and said, "Did you travel through the spooky forest of Night?"

"Yes," said Nugget.

"Along the Shore of Eeriness, next to the Sea of Despair?"

"Yes!"

"Then through the valley of Darkness and follow the track through the Land of Doom?"

"Yes."

"Did you then take a left and find the Cave of Tremendous Peril?"

"Yes."

"And were you ever harmed at any point?"

The horse thought for a while.

"Errrrr, no, not really."

"And what made you frightened in the first place?"

"Well, it's the names, ain't it! I mean they sound so frightening!"

"Uhm. And you and Sir Terrence survived unscathed didn't you?"

"Well, er, yes."

"Exactly! Fear is merely in the mind," said the Court Physician, who was very wise and clever, by the way.

"So, er, what exactly lives in this cave?" asked Terrence.

"Oh, I don't know... Bats, or rats, or something..." said the physician.

"Might it have two massive, leathery wings?"

"Possibly..."

"A big, tall head with spiky horns?"

"Potentially..."

"Have a long, scaly tail?"

"Maybe..."

"Breath fire through its nostrils and have large, yellow eyes, that look evil and menacing?"

"It's quite conceivable..."

"Why?" asked Nugget. "Coz I don't like the sound of something that has two massive, leathery wings, a big, tall head with spiky horns, a long scaly tail and breathes fire through its nostrils, have large, yellow eyes that look evil and menacing."

"What, er, what would something like that description be, possibly, potentially, maybe?" asked Terrence.

"What? Something that has two massive, leathery wings, a

big, tall head with spiky horns, a long scaly tail and breathes fire through its nostrils, have large, yellow eyes that look evil and menacing? What might that be? Er, I think that would be a dragon."

"A dragon?" said Nugget.

"A dragon?" said Terrence.

"Yes, a dragon," said the Court Physician. "Why?"

"Er, because, because it's right behind you..."

All three of them screamed.

"Aargh!!!"

Then the fearless three ran all the way back to the castle, taking the short cut, by the way.

Along their journey, they ran through a farmer's field which housed many horses, which led Nugget to enquire of whom they were. So he wandered over to them and heard one horse that seemed particularly distressed...

PATIENCE.

"Ooo! Ouch!"

"What's wrong?" said the foal to its father.

"I've a really bad pain in my foot and it's really hurting me."

Father Horse lay down trying to nurse his poorly hoof. Nudging it, the foal accidentally set his dad off on another round of groans and aches.

"I'll go and get help," said the foal and trotted off to find someone who could assist.

"Umm, let me think," said Ernest the shire horse.

"I think I know what the problem is."

So the two trotted back to see father horse.

"You have something we horses call, Thornithurtus. See that thorn there? We need to remove it," said Ernest. So he went off to get help.

The foal continued to think about how he could help her dad. More groans and exclamations were heard, so she wandered off to find help again.

"Umm," said the goat. "Thornithurtus, eh? Maybe try bathing it in water."

So the foal found a small bowl of water and pushed it towards her father, but this didn't help. So again she went off to get assistance.

"Oh, Thornithurtus, eh?" said the sheep.

"Take some straw and see if binding the hoof with it helps."

So the foal gathered some straw and took it to her father and tried to cushion the hoof, but it just made the horse laugh as it trickled his feet. Again, the foal went off to get help but the father horse told his daughter not to worry, for the shire horse would get help.

"Have a little patience; the shire horse will be back soon with the right help."

Yet the young foal was determined to bring relief to her dad's poorly foot and went off again.

"Oh dear, Thornithurtus, eh? That's a tricky one. Try getting some grass and cushion the hoof with it."

So the foal gathered some grass and took it to her dad, but it didn't work, nor feel any better.

"Patience, my girl! Wait for the shire horse will you!"

Yet again though, the foal went away so try and find help.

"Thornithurtus?! Now that's nasty! Have you tried water?" asked the cow.

"Yes."

"Straw?"

"Yes."

"Grass?"

"Yes."

"Right. Have you tried taking the thorn out with your teeth?"

"No."

So the foal went back and tried to take out the thorn out with its teeth. Amidst the laughs from having ticklish feet and the cries of pain as the foal tried to remove the thorn, father horse said, "Stop, stop! I don't know whether to laugh or cry! Have patience daughter and wait for the shire horse!"

"Someone mention my name?" asked the shire horse.

In trotted the large horse with the farmer following behind.

"What have we here? A thorn in the hoof? Very nasty! One moment and I'll get it sorted," said the farmer and he went away then returned with certain sundries. Then he knelt down and removed the thorn gently and cleaned the wound. Afterwards, he placed a shoe on the horse's hoof with some fur around the edges so it would cushion the foot.

"Thank you," said the father horse.

"See, my daughter, it just goes to show that patience is a fur-shoe."

"I thought it was a virtue," said Ernest the shire horse.

"It is," replied father horse.

"But it's also a fur-shoe."

One might think that the same may apply to what happening close by, for a creature was squawked quite loudly, day and night, trying the patience of many beasts, birds and other beings...

The White Peacock.

A beautiful, white peacock graced the land within the bounds of Darque's kingdom. It had speckles of light brown within its feathers that radiated a golden glow and some of the feather-tips had the same auric glow.

"Kaur-orr! Kaur-orr," it would cry, attracting the attention of passers-by.

On one such occasion, a nobleman was passing through the Darque kingdom. He heard the bird's call and saw the peacock in flight, landing near to him and became entranced. At once he wanted to find the owner, so to ask if he could have it. Following information from a farmer, he went to the village elder, who pointed him in the Duke's direction, who directed the nobleman to the king. Alas, the king was not present in his hall, so the nobleman went away, coveting the white peacock.

The bird filled his dreams and daydreams, taking up all his mental time and becoming his main distraction. Taking leave, he ventured back to the Darque kingdom, determined to acquire the peacock. How splendid it would look on his land, in his garden! He imagined how people would be amazed at the beautiful bird.

Finding the king in his residence, he sought court with him, to which he was warmly invited.

"Your highness! I could not help notice the wonderful peacock that you have on your land and, I must confess, I covet it. It is so beautiful, so majestic, with its white feathers flecked with gold. Forgive my impertinence, but how much, or what would you require of me, that I could own this magnificent bird?"

The king looked at the nobleman with surprise, shocked by the bold request.

"Because of your boldness, you may have the white peacock, which I acquired from the Indias. Please accept, for such a brave request must surely be rewarded and I require no reciprocation."

The nobleman smiled and beamed, announcing his appreciation. Collecting his prize, without any cost, was greatly appreciated by the nobleman and the courtiers arranged for a suitable crate to house the bird safely for its journey. As he travelled back home, the bird called out, "Kaur-orr! Kaur-orr!"

The king of Darque watched from a turret, observing the departure of his guest. Once the nobleman and the peacock were far away, he descended back to his hall and smiled at his Queen saying, "Thank goodness we got rid of that barking bird! I was sick and tired of its racket!!"

"It was driving me insane," said the Queen. "I'm so glad we're rid of it! Isn't it peculiar that one person's desire can be another's insanity?"

FAITH AND MARMALADE.

"Now then, young Puddles, we are going to take a look at faith."

Collecting Puddles from his meditation training, he brought him back to his home for another valuable lesson.

"Faith?"

"Yes, faith. The belief and ability to trust in a future outcome. We shall start by opening this door."

The cats looked at the big white living room door that was keeping them from going into the hallway.

"So first," said Marmalade, "picture the door in your mind and then picture it as if it is already open."

"Er, okay."

"No 'er'. Have no doubt! Don't question it. Trust your vision!"

"Right..."

Puddles stared blankly at the door and appeared slightly vacant.

"Are you visualizing the open door?"

"Wye aye."

"Have you any doubt? Is there any suspicion, any stirring of negativity there, lurking in the dark recesses of the mind? Is there? IS THERE?"

"No, man!"

"Good! Then act as though the door is open..."

Puddles stood up rather abruptly and ran head first into the closed door. Marmalade looked at the young tabby with confusion.

"What the chuff are you doing?"

"Acting as if the door's open, like ye said!"

"But it's not open!"

"Aye, but you said to act as if it were already open!"

"I know that! But the door HAS to actually be open yer great nincompoop!"

"I was only doing what you said!"

"Yes, that's great, but I think you need to have the door actually open first, don't you? Eh? Otherwise this exercise will lead you to a concussion. Maybe we should get you some sort of helmet..."

Puddles slumped back to resting on the floor, blinking his eyes and shaking his head to put himself right.

"Right, let's try again shall we? Visualize the door openING, openING, okay? Is it open? Is that young brain working? Cast out any doubt! Cast asunder the negativity! And let the door open...!"

There was a pause to allow the grand opening of the living room door. Alas, nothing happened. Marmalade's eyes were wide in expectation, vividly watching for any activity, any sign, any hint of movement. Nothing. The white, wooden door remained closed.

"Miaow ow miaow, errh mao!" yelled Puddles.

"What are you doing?" asked a bemused and unamused Marmalade.

"Wait, man."

A sudden rush of what ported to be an elephant came clattering down the stairs and then the door opened.

"Ah! Hello Puddles. Is this your friend? Do you wanna go upstairs?" said a human voice, the voice of a child called, Mia.

"Mao."

"Come on then..."

Marmalade stared at Puddles with a look that was close to contempt.

"Now that's cheating."

"Aye, maybe. But I nahs it works. I had faith they'd come and open it."

"Still cheating in my book..."

"Is the door open? Wye aye."

"You're a cheat."

"Nah. It's knowing it would open."

"Umm."

THE INVISIBLE FRIEND.   *(For Mia)*

On a farm, somewhere in the countryside, was a large farm house. Upstairs in the house was Mia, a young girl who had an invisible friend and what a naughty friend it was. It would take out all the toys, dressing up costumes and shoes and leave them all over. Mia's mum would ask, "And who made all this mess?" Mia would reply, "It's Amy! She did it."

Now, one day Amy went too far and broke an ornament that was loved by her mum. Mia did not know how it had happened.

"Can you ask Amy what happened, for me please?"

"Yes," said Mia and asked Amy what had happened to the precious ornament. Mia listened and said, "Amy says that as she was putting on the princess dress, her arm got stuck in the sleeve. So she pushed it through and accidentally knocked over the ornament. But Amy also says she is very sorry, mum."

"Well, that's okay. It's a shame it happened, but it's only an ornament. I'm sure we can get another one."

After this, the invisible friend started reminding Mia of all the things she had done wrong, so much so that she began to cry each time. Amy reminded her of these things because Mia had blamed Amy for breaking the ornament and this upset her. She reminded Mia of when she hurt her friend Sophie, when Mia stole a chocolate bar; the time Mia broke her dad's favourite mug and many more things.

One day Mia was crying when her dad found her. She explained how Amy was being nasty and knew everything naughty that she'd ever done.

"Hmm," said dad. "Well, why don't you keep a bowl of rice next to your bed and next time she says anything nasty, go grab a handful of rice from the bowl, without counting how many grains and ask Amy how many grains of rice you have in your hand."

So next time Amy was nasty and reminded Mia of when she had been naughty, Mia ran out to the drive and picked up a hand full of stones. "How many are in my hand?" she asked, but Amy could not answer. Whenever Amy was nasty, Mia did the same and asked how many stones she held in her hand.

Eventually, Amy stopped hanging around Mia and the house became a lot tidier and not so many things were broken.

"Where's Amy these days?" asked mum.

"Oh, I don't play with her anymore," said Mia. "Invisible friends aren't as good as real ones."

Now Mia had a brother called, Thomas, who did very well at school and on one occasion had won a trophy...

The Hamster.

On the windowsill in his bedroom was the trophy. He had won the trophy for being the best student in his class. On the plaque underneath, the name, Thomas had been etched and it stood proudly to remind him of success. Thomas had a friend, Adam, who was jealous of him and the trophy. Whenever Adam was around he would say to himself, "I wish that trophy was mine!"

One day, Adam called at Thomas' house, but he wasn't in. So Adam went upstairs and went in the bedroom, saw the trophy and took it. Now, as it had the name of Thomas on it, Adam knew that he could not ever show it or put it as proudly on display as Thomas had, so he put it in a box.

One day Thomas went way to see Adam. When Thomas arrived at Adam's home, he noticed a new box in his room. "What's in the box?" asked Thomas.

"Er, it's er, it's my hamster, he died I'm afraid and I was unsure what to do with him, but didn't want to look at him so placed him in the box."

"I'm sorry to hear that. What we should do is bury him; give him a special burial," said Thomas.

So the two boys took the box to the back field and buried it and no more was ever said. The field housed livestock like horses, cows, sheep and goats and it is in the goat's abode where our next story takes place...

THE BOSSY GOAT.

Gertrude was getting on in years and the slightly younger, mother goats put up with her. One she-goat in particular, Jess, would help the old goat though and had the patience to do so, as Gertrude was extremely bossy.

"I need more hay!"
"I'm hungry! Get me food!"
"Tell that kid to stop hopping about; it's getting on my nerves."
"Not here but there."
"No, no that one, the OTHER One!"

These were just some of the things Gertrude would say to Jess. The other goats would ask Jess, "How can you put up with that? She's dreadful and so bossy. How do you deal with it?"

"It's in the way we react to people like Gertrude that matters. If you tell Gertrude to 'do it herself,' it starts an argument. However, if you respond with kindness and the right attitude, it means she will actually listen to what you have to say. So, it's not how I put up with Gertrude, but how I respond to her."

Gertrude was aware that she was growing closer to the day when she would depart this world and as the matriarch of the goats, she would have to find a replacement for her position. Many of the other she-goats were of the same age, so they all jostled for the position. They seemed to stop being nasty about each other, so to become the embodiment of good virtues.

"It's funny how attitudes change when opportunities arise," said Gertrude, as she looked about for a suitable replacement to take her role. "I have made my decision and it is none of you lot!"

The she-goats gasped and wondered who would become the matriarch. Jess, who was one of the younger goats, was summoned to the group.

"I have chosen Jess to be my successor, for she is the kindest and wisest goat I know. She also has a pleasant disposition, which is considerably more constant, as opposed to the shifting attitudes of you lot! So Jess will replace me."

The she-goats started to moan and rolled their eyes at the situation. Gertrude hushed them all by saying, "And if any of you lot give Jess grief in this life, well, I'll be sure to sort you out in the next!"

MARMALADE'S MEMOIR.

Twice upon a certain point in space-time, in a certain galaxy, on a particular planet, somewhere on a continent, in a country, at another time, in another place, someone was doing something, or maybe nothing in particular. On the first instance it was nothing, but the second time it occurred it was really something; amazing, first class, top notch and fantastic, yet a certain 'thing' was missing. This was because the 'thing' was still at the first instance, trying to make sense of it all, whatever it was that happened, hence the need for it to happen again, so some comprehension could be gained by some means, somehow. Yet everyone thought, "What's he going on about? Is he bonkers, completely off his chunk? Has he become a total nut-job?" And this is where I, your humble host come in, to help all understand what the bloomin' heck is going on. So I shall endeavour to explain it to you, somehow, by some means, in some fashion. My preference is via the medium of the written word.

Many moons ago, well not literal moons as there's just the one moon, but I'm alluding to the passage of time, so really I should have said, 'A long time ago,' but everyone says that and I was trying to be different, but now I've stated that I was trying to be different I actually sound unoriginal, thus I've negated my opening I feel, but anyway, I digress. A long time ago, I was born. I remember it distinctly, it was a Tuesday, no a Thursday, well it began with 'T' anyway, and it was around 12 minutes past 8 in the morning on a sunny, yet autumnal day in June. On this grand occasion I came forth from the womb and took a breath then thought, 'What's happened? Where am I? Who am I? Who turned the light on? Who's licking me?' Then I wriggled around a bit and settled down next to my mother, Tigerlily. Yes, I am a catlet. Did I not mention that? I'm a cat, my name, Marmalade. They were going to call me Tinky-Winky, but thankfully I was saved from this catastrophe, but I feel the next thing you're probably asking yourself is, how can a cat write? Well, in the past some clever chap invented a thing called type-writer and this idea evolved into something known as a word-processor, or computer and I, being a genius, observed humans using them then assimilated this and learnt the human language known as English, as well as my native Catanese, so I could eventually convey my story to you, the reader, writing this with my very own paws. So, anyway, like I said, I was born and raised along with 8 others by my mother. I never knew my father. I did try to find him but however valiantly I searched, I failed. Anyway, I'm going off the point a tad so will endeavour to head back on the path which is the story I describe to you now.

From a young age I was taught how to clean myself, flex my claws, flick my tail and be a catlet. That was until one day when I was very rudely taken from the comfort of my mother and undertook a long journey to Shoreham By Sea, where I was whisked away on a large boat and ended up in some deserted little town somewhere in the middle Americas. It was a bloomin' awful place called, Pity, and yes, *what a pity it was,* for it could have been so much more! It had a lovely little street with a few houses, a general stores, a church and a donkey called, Harold. They could have branched out and had a railroad station, a telegraph office, a doctor, dentist, an osteopath and nice cafes with those little tables outside with doilies on and those tiny flower vases holding a singular buttercup.

I'm sorry. I digress again. Where was I? Ah, yes, so I lived with a woman called Dorothea, until I felt this urge, the feeling to explore whatever lay outside the front door. And so one day I went and travelled far and wide, ending up in a wonderful, mystical place known as, Rocky Comfort. And yes, it's comfort was rather rocky! In fact it was so rocky that the fulcrum had swayed completely towards the uncomfortable balance of the equation. Anyway, there I was, alone in Balboa's bosom and shacked up with some other catlets in a kitten kibbutz who were under the auspices of a guru type cat person called, Tipsy. I know it doesn't sound very spiritual does it eh? Tipsy? Guru Tipsy? I think I would've renamed myself more appropriate and suitable. Alas, 'twas not the case in this instance and Guru Tipsy began to teach us about the world and things that would help us live a peaceful life by way of tales, fables, parables and poetic, prose type things that are neither poems or stories, but somewhere in between. And some of them did go on - boy, did they go on! I remember one in particular called, Bugva the Bloomin' 'Orrible, and yes, it was bloomin' horrible, going on about this and that, and not really leading anywhere, with no real narrative or clear objective leading to a conclusion. It was absolutely dreadfull! How anyone can write such aimless drivel is beyond me. Now, where was I?

Right then, so I was with this guru type person and I learnt a lot from him, yet I longed for more, as if there was something missing from my appetite for life. I didn't know what it was I was searching for, what the missing ingredient was. So I set about on my travels once more and ventured to stranger environs. I went to Japan, South Korea, China, Tibet then Nepal to research some inner mysteries of spirituality. After this, I went through India to then I ran. I ran. Then I Raquel. (I'm sorry, that should be Iran but the computer's predictive text thinks it knows better. No matter how many times I type it, it keeps thinking I was running after someone called Raquel.) Anyway, after visiting the former Mesopotamian empire, I ventured to Armenia, the Holy Land, Jordan & Egypt. On these travels I absorbed the cultures (not bacteria I hasten to add), ways, religious beliefs, foods and the one thing that permeated through all these findings was the reality of a supernatural and the magic that is faith. I also found that jasmine tea mixed with hibiscus is utterly revolting and that Yak's milk is wonderful. However, the high fat content plays merry hell with my cholesterol, so I'm consequently on Cat-statins and a low fat diet, which means I consume low lactose cheese & yoghurts, lots of cereal and a kibble known as, Cheeky Chunks, which is devoid of any flavour other than cardboard. I've never eaten cardboard, except that one time when I was fooled by a female cat called, Brunhilda, into trying a new kind of rice paper. It was a practical joke that went horribly wrong and my poop ending up looking like it was pre-wrapped in some bizarre yet rigid toilet tissue. Suffice to say, nothing stuck to my fur, which was a blessing, but I developed an insatiable appetite for rye bread & crackers with capers & anchovies as a result. Anyway, getting back to my point, I travelled far and wide, except through certain parts of Europe. Why? I'll tell you chuffin' why; those infuriating mime artists. Yes, them that moves within the confines of a glass box which isn't really there. Their lack of vocalisation means they contort their faces like a gurning buffoon which annoys me even further. Then to top it all off, they end by pulling them self off the stage via an invisible rope, that quite frankly I wish was hanging around a certain part of their anatomy until it brought some sanity into their lives. Bloomin' mimes - they perturb me to the highest degree.. Suffice to say, I hardly ever travel through certain European, continental countries that harvest this art form, only to unleash it when I am nearby. Some people don't like clowns, well I don't like mimes!

My apologies again for diverging down a cul-de-sac not relevant to the journey of our story. Moving on, I arrived at what ports to be a type of enlightenment. It occurred around 2.30pm on Wednesday 15th July in the year something-or-other and it was a moment of exquisite discernment and clarity leading to a sense of calm euphoria. It was if everything fell into place, the final pieces of the jigsaw found their locations, the bee had found the nectar, the lover had found the beloved, which was awfully nice. I think it's a common misconception though, that once a person, or cat, has this intellectual satori and amazing awakening, that life is never the same again, that it is somewhat easier. Well, I can tell that it's not. In fact, the old proverb says, "Before enlightenment, chop wood & fetch water – after enlightenment, chop wood & fetch water," and it's absolutely correct. You achieve a state of grace, serenity and patience, but believe me, you still encounter those known as chuffin' half-wits, you know, those people who can't even open a bag of cat litter with left-handed scissors, due to the fact that they're actually using an ice-cream scoop, yes, and I wouldn't be eating any Choccy-Toffee-Choo-Choo ice-cream served by them, I can tell you! Goodness knows what you'd be chewing... Yes, these are the type of people who purchase paint for those who are on diets, as the hue makes them look slimmer; those who look at their right hand when you tell them to, 'turn left here;' the one who pushes a door that has 'Pull' written in big letters on the door itself, or thinks they're a genius because they realise that 'out' means the same as 'not in;' who swallows bubble-gum in the hope they'll blow bubbles with their bottom and who looks at you like you're the idiot when you've answered the question they asked, but they haven't heard the answer they needed to hear, like, "Did you put the bins out?"

"Yes, I put the bins out."

"Did you put the blue bin out?"

"Yes, I put the bins out, as I've just told you!"

"But the blue bin is emptied every other week, except when there's an 'r' in the month, so make sure it's out."

"I already told you, I've put the bins out!"

"Yes, but is the blue bin out, or it'll be 2 weeks before it's emptied again."

"Look, I told you, I put the bins out!!"

"And the blue one?"

"Yes!!! I've put the bins out, including the blue one!" "Well, that's all you had to say."

Now, I know not everyone has been blessed with their faculties filled to the brim, such as when one has counted another's deck of cards and found it wanting, but we all know them, these type of people, don't we?

No matter how spiritual, enlightened or awake you may be, you will always meet these personages and when we do meet those who challenge us, the situation can only be overcome by forgiveness, extending grace and being patient. Anyway, so yes, getting back to my point, I achieved a grand awakening, that kensho moment, a while ago and it was rather nice.

Now I expect you are all wondering, where I'm going with this meandering of memories as we march forward in time, well basically I'm giving you a bit of an autobiography about moi, the moggy known as Marmalade. I know it is a little self-indulgent, but aren't we allowed to be, just a little bit, from time to time, eh? The main thrust of my memoir is to explain that we all have inner urges and often feel that something is missing from our lives. Often that missing thing is part of our spiritual self. Moreover, it is not a place with a physical location that we seek, but a location within ourselves that helps to find our deep inner peace. Thus my hope is that the rich tapestry of tales I have compiled for you, dear reader, leads you to a deeper understanding of how we can each live our lives by learning from our experiences, anecdotes and the shared stories that teach us aspects of how to live, that have been shared between, continents, countries, cultures & beliefs since the dawn of catlets, doglings, humans and all life. These tales change according to the time, surroundings and culture but there is an integrity that remains inherent within, teaching us the same today as it did yesterday and will tomorrow, until all our tomorrows become yesterdays, the future becomes the past and the past but an eternal moment in the museum of consciousness that exists within our little corner of the universe. And when the time comes for the star to explode in the midst of our galaxy, bringing our galactic neighbourhood to an end, these recycled moments and memories will become an intrinsic part of space-time telling the tale of our experience to the ancient, timeless one who some call God, or maybe the source, universe or the cosmos, who will ask, "How was it then?"

The answer? "Well, it was certainly an experience! Do you have anything else? Maybe in another galaxy somewhere? In a size 10? Maybe in a nice beige?"

The universe will then smile and lead us to the next stage of existence, guiding us in and letting us play & dance, like specs of dust dancing in the light and I will say, "Well you could have dusted! Look at all that dust floating about the place. It'll trigger my allergies, y'know. Now where's a duster? I'll get cleaning straight away! For a non-corporeal entity, you're not very tidy are you?" I'm sure I heard a titter there... Maybe I've amused the cosmic entity and it's laughing at me. I hope so, for it always helps to have a giggle and not be overly serious. After all, we have to enjoy life, don't we? Even if I have to take antihistamines! For let us not forget, that everything and everyone ever created has stardust within them. Actually, I think that may mean I'm allergic to existence... Oh, I'm going to sneeze, you'll have to excuse me.

Bless me!

Now where was I? Oh, yes; once there was a mighty warrior who happened across an old man in a public house...

THE GREATEST WARRIOR.

There was a certain soldier who gained popularity by winning every fight he had. In battle, he killed 10 times more people than others in his regiment. One day he came up against an old man, who was drinking in a public house. The old man had done nothing to the soldier, but merely chuckled silently as the soldier boasted of his victories. The soldier noticed and challenged him to a fight. So they went outside to fight. The soldier launched at the old man, who merely stepped out of his way. Getting up from the ground, the soldier took a stance and went to strike the man who dodged the blow, then the next and the next. Infuriated, the soldier grabbed the man's wrist and went to wrestle him, but the old man moved his wrist in the direction the soldier was moving and slipped the grasp. Now the soldier was even angrier and got three other men to hold him whilst he punched him until he was black and blue.

"I see it takes four men to beat me, not one," said the old man and in that moment, everyone around heard and the soldier was defeated. Taking the matter to heart, the soldier realized he had indeed been beaten and apologized profusely to the old man.

"How did you become a mighty warrior?" the soldier asked.

"I learnt to fight as a young man and won many tournaments. Unsatisfied, I went to find the mightiest fighter and beat him, but still I was not satisfied. So one day, I asked the sage where I could find the victory that would satisfy my thirst. He told me to go up into the hills, find the oldest tree and there I would find him. Once I defeated him, I was to return. So I went, and now I tell you the same. Go there and fight the warrior by the oldest tree in the hills, and do not return until he is defeated."

So the soldiers went. He travelled for many days until he found the oldest tree in the hills. Once he found it, he saw no one. From the hilltop, he viewed the countryside, but no one was nearby. Not wanting to appear stupid, he realised he needed to stay a while, so everyone would think he had this amazing victory, then he could return. So he sat under the tree and as he looked out, he saw that nearby was a natural pond and beside it a small, wooden post with a sign. Venturing over to it, he read the little sign which read, "The Mighty Warrior." The soldier looked at the pond, splashed the water, walked in it, but found no one. Feeling confused, he sat beside the pond and as the water settled, he saw his reflection. He thought for a while and said to himself, "How can I fight a reflection? Furthermore, how can I fight myself?" Not wanting to appear stupid, he sat back down and thought about what he would say to people to explain how he won the fight. As he did so, he realized he could not. An answer to his question eluded him and at this point he admitted defeat. The pond had won the battle, for he could not fight it, nor defeat his own reflection. Without a single blow, the water had defeated him. So, he resolved to go back and find the old man and tell him.

"What did you find?" quizzed the man.

"Only water and my own reflection," replied the soldier. "I had no fight, for you cannot fight water or yourself!"

"On the contrary," said the old man, "Your greatest foe is yourself and you could not win, so who has won in this battle of your mind? Thus, you overcame yourself to be the greatest warrior, and you never struck one blow."

The soldier became silent. Slowly, his frown became a smile and the soldier began to laugh.

"Tell me, who told you about the pond up in the hills?"

"Well, a long time ago, there was a man called Storm, who grew up in a time of great threat..."

STORM THE CONQUEROR.

The neighbouring kingdom threatened to conquer the land where he lived. Storm trained as a soldier and quickly arose through the ranks, until he eventually became a general. He was entrusted by the queen to act on her behalf, even without her say, for such was his wisdom. He won every battle and war he had been in, and led such trust that whatever he said could be approved without the queen being present. As such, he became the queen's chief advisor.

The neighbouring kingdom's threat still overshadowed the land and eventually the king ordered that they conquer the queen's territories. So, the king sent 3 men to the queendom to take a message, relinquish or be overthrown. The 3 never returned with an answer. So, the king sent 13 skilled negotiators with a message, kneel before the king and live, or be conquered. After a month, the 13 had not returned and all hope was lost at hearing from them. The king then sent 30 fine warriors with a message, be conquered or submit. Yet, the 30 never returned. The king was unsure as what to do, so he sent 300 men to fight the queen's men and also relay the message of submit or be conquered. None of the 300 returned. This had the king mighty vexed, so he sends 3000 men in the same manner, only this time, he sends 3 spies with them, to see what happens. Lo and behold, the 3000 do not return and only one spy returns.

"What goes on? What happens to my men?"

"Er, well, see, there's this man who has the queen's hand. He's called, Storm. When anyone enters the land, they are taken before him and he questions them and most are never seen of again! Some say he eats them, but others say he burns them alive. Yet others say he fights them one by one, for such a strong fighter is he. And more say he buries them alive until they confess their true intentions."

"And what do you say? What have you seen?" asked the king.

"I saw only two men enter the palace and neither returned or left. I heard no screams, saw no smoke, heard no torture or saw any torment. I say it is most strange and ask you to carefully consider what you will do, for such is his renown, his strength and devotion to the queen."

The king thought about it long and hard, deciding to seek advice of his trusted advisors. Soon it was decided, he would send 30,000 to take the border and wage battle.

And the men went to battle, all 30,000. The king watched from a distance, to see what came to pass. The men were matched by 30,000 of the queen's men and before the battle, an emissary went to the king's men from the queen, bearing the queen's standard and a message. Much to the king's disgust, there was no battle, no blood, no war. In a rage, he took his horse to the border and stormed onto the queen's land, but some of the queen's guards stopped him and caused him to dismount.

"I demand to see the queen's hand!"

So, the guards took him before Storm. He sat alone in a large, dark room, bathed only in lamp light. At the far end sat Storm, on a princely throne. The king was trembling, unsure what to do. Would he suffer the same fate as his many men? As he approached the throne, his armour rattled with nerves, until the suspense could not be bared anymore. The shadow of Storm leant over the now kneeling king.

"Do with me what you will, but spare my country, spare my people!"

Storm silently stood up and walked over a few paces to the king. "And why should I do that? You have tried to conquer us for many years! Why should I spare your kingdom?"

"You are right, I have sought to overthrow your queendom, but I surrender to you. Spare me family, my kith, my people!"

"I shall offer you the same as I have offered everyone else," said Storm. "But if you surrender, well that's different altogether!"

The king didn't know what to say or do.

"So do you surrender? Or do you want the offer I made to the 3, the 13, the 30, the 300, the 3,000 and the 30,000? Well?"

Storm awaited an answer. Finally, the king answered, "I submit before you, surrender to your queen. Do with me as you will, but do not harm anymore of my men!"

"Very well. The queen accepts your surrender. Go into the next chamber and await your fate."

The king moved to the chamber, relieved that the ordeal was over. He moved through the chamber and was greeted by a prison warden who led him to a cell.

Days passed and the king could not help wonder what had happened to his men. Such was his curiosity that he asked the warden if he may speak to the queen.

The queen decided to visit the king in his cell, viewing him from behind the iron gate.

"What fate befell my men? My 3, my 13, my 30, my 3,000, my 30,000?" asked the king.

"Oh, they are safe and well."

"How? Did not Storm kill them, eat them? Bury some alive?"

"No, not one of them."

"Then what became of them?"

The queen smiled and said, "We offered each of them land, a home, freedom and peace in their lifetime. We told them to fetch their families here also once the tyrant had been imprisoned. Lo, behold, here you are! And this is how I conquered your kingdom."

"Where did you learn of this wisdom? "

"When I was a child, my father would take me around the city and he had a good friend, Rishi, who owned a quarry. Everyone thought it odd, that a commoner was good friends with a king, but this never bothered my father. He would ask Rishi to tell me the stories that he had been told when my father was a youth, so he did. And one of those stories was about how Rishi once hired a man for some work..."

THE MOUNTAIN THAT MOVED.

A sign hung outside the office reading, "Labourer wanted urgently." Many saw the sign, but few enquired within to take up the offer, that was until Mo entered the office.

"How much will you pay?"

"Once the work is completed, I will pay you £150."

"That is fine with me; show me the task!"

Rishi, the boss, took Mo out the back of the office to a yard, where a mountain of rubble lay. At once, Mo frowned and appeared perturbed by the task at hand. Not moaning, he asked, "What needs doing?"

"I need that mountain moving over there, please."

Rishi pointed to a space roughly 100 metres away, at the other side of the yard, then handed Mo a shovel. Next to where he stood was a rusty, old wheelbarrow, and Mo placed the shovel in it and went over to the mountain. He thought to himself, "This will take forever! I wish I had never agreed to this." Nevertheless, he set to work.

Each time he filled the barrow, Mo moved it across then emptied it. After four journeys, his back began to ache. He carried on and after twelve journeys, his arms began to ache also. It seemed as if he had barely touched the mound and became disheartened. All the time he was doing this, Mo noticed a snail in the corner of the yard, heading towards the cabbages. Every now and again, he looked towards the snail as he shovelled the rubble. After the first day's work, Mo looked at the mountain and thought about how little he had done. Next day, he continued as before, taking each barrowful from one place to the other, but at the end of the day, again he thought about how little he had done. After the third day, Mo approached Rishi and explained that he felt he was not up to the task.

"This will take me forever and I no longer think I am able to do this."

"You will be fine. Eat, sleep, rest and comeback tomorrow."

So Mo ate his meal then went to bed. He returned next day and carried on with his labour. His enthusiasm was diminishing which meant he became slower in his task. Rishi came out to see how Mo was doing.

"Good, good! You are almost a quarter of the way there."

"Yes, but I've three quarters left to go! My back hurts, my arms hurt, my legs ache and the sun is beating at my head."

"Pah! You are still moving, so carry on."

"The task is too difficult, I want to quit!"

"Quit? Never! You're doing so well. I won't let you go. Besides, who will finish moving the mountain?"

"Anyone but me!"

"Pah! You are going to finish this."

"The mountain is never to be moved! It's too great a job."

Looking towards the cabbages, Rishi noticed the snail nearing it. "You see the snail?"

"Yes," said Mo. "The other day it was over by the rubble."

"When you look at the snail, it doesn't seem to move, but when you don't watch it, it does move. How is this?"

Mo thought about this for a moment.

"Well, the snail is always moving, it's just that when observing it, it seems not to move."

"It's just like the mountain; don't look at the size of it, just focus on the task. You're thinking about how big it is when you should be focusing on merely moving it."

Pondering this, Mo began to carry on shovelling the rocks. He began to focus on merely moving the mountain.

"Don't think about the end, consider only the action of moving it," said Rishi as he walked away. And Mo began to focus on just shovelling and emptying rubble to and from the wheelbarrow.

"I'm hungry, hurting and sunburnt," stated Mo when Rishi came back to him.

"Don't think about how you feel, focus on moving rocks."

"But my back is breaking!"

"Pay no attention to that, think only on what you are doing."

"But it's agony!"

"Pain is just a thought. Stop thinking and practice doing what you are doing. Focus only on the mountain."

Once more, Rishi walked away. As he entered the hut, he noticed the snail climbing up to a cabbage, its horns moving excitedly.

On the 7th day, Rishi came back to the yard. The snail was munching its way through the cabbage and the sun was beating down on Mo's back and head. As Rishi came to view the mountain of rubble, he noticed that it had been moved and that Mo had completed the task. A large smile grew on Rishi's face. He began counting out the money as promised to Mo from the outset.

"Well done! There you go, there's your money. Thank you for your services. I had faith in your ability."

"You're welcome," said a very tired Mo and with that, he began to walk away. Rishi followed after him and went to the front of the little office. As Mo left, Rishi placed a sign up on the door, 'Labourer wanted urgently.' Mo looked back to see the sign back up, so soon. He went back over to Rishi and said, "What work needs doing now?"

"Oh, I need that mountain of rubble moving."

"Why? I just moved it!"

"I will pay you £100 to do the task."

"You only paid me £150 before! What do you mean by this?"

"Well, if you do it this time, you will learn more."

Mo laughed out loud.

"Pay me nothing and teach me everything!"

"Okay. Now move that mountain from there to here. This time using only your own faith."

So Mo sat down and thought about it. Rishi patted him on the shoulder, saying, "Don't think about it, just do it. Believe you can do it, just as I believed you could."

Mo bowed his head and wiped his brow.

"Teacher, teach me how!"

Rishi looked at Mo then said, "Listen and hear what I say, pay attention..

THE LOVE THIEVES.   *(For Martin)*

There was once a young woman had a gift that she wished to give another, yet no one wanted it. It was a message of love, but no one wanted to receive it. She became so upset, that she approached her father for advice.

"Do not upset yourself my child, if no one wants to hear your message of love, keep it until the right person asks for it," said her father.

"I cannot keep it, for it longs to be shared. All of those I have tried to give it to listen but do not take it to their heart."

"Then write it down, bind it so it can be easily opened, then leave it under the moon. On top of the book, write, 'Do not remove,' and surely the right person will take it."

So the daughter wrote a little book to contain the message, bound it lightly and then went out into the night, placing it under the moon. Resting on top was a sign, "Please do not remove."

The next morning, she went to see if the book was where she had left it, but it had gone. Excitedly, she told her father about the book being gone.

"My child, sometimes people do not want what is freely given, yet tell someone that they cannot have it and they begin to covet it."

"Why is this, father?"

"It is indeed very curious. It is the nature of humankind to want that which is free, yet some feel the gain of taking what is not theirs, for to them it has greater value. Either way, it is free, for nothing is truly ours, but given on lease, such as life, love and the air we breathe."

No Mistakes.

There was a young man who read many books. One night, as he was walking, he stumbled upon a package, which was a book, so took it home with him. He read it and thought, "Hmm, brilliant! Now I know all about love."

Now this young man claimed to know about everything he had read and was able to do anything, just because he had read about it. In fact, when it came to fixing something, he could do so, by reading a book about it. One day it was discovered that the things he had fixed were still not working properly, so he visited the elder.

"I have never made a mistake, but the water pump still does not work. I have read all the books on fixing it, but still it does not work."

The village elder said, "Then you have made a mistake, if the pump still does not work."

"I never make mistakes!"

"Just because you have read the books, doesn't mean you know how to fix it."

"No, the pump must be broken, no good; I never make mistakes!"

"Well," said the elder, "You must be a genius! To be able to read everything and fix everything simply by reading books, that is genius! So why does the water pump still not work?"

"It is unfixable. We need a new one."

"On the contrary, we need a someone else to fix the pump! If my table is broken, I go to a carpenter. If my roof is leaking, I seek a builder; if my clothes need stitching, I go to a someone who can sew. Yet you are a carpenter, builder, seamstress and more? Fetch me a plumber and we shall fix the water pump!"

Chagrined, the young man relented and sought a plumber, who came and fixed the pump. The plumber took one look at it and saw the problem and fixed it. The young man felt deflated.

"I am amazed that the unfixable is fixed," said the elder.

"Well... The books never mentioned about that part the plumber replaced."

"This is your first mistake. We learn by making mistakes, not just by reading. An educated person makes mistakes just as an uneducated person does. Go away and make mistakes, then come back to me and tell me what you have learnt."

So the young man went away, feeling disheartened, so much so, that it was noticed by his friend.

"Why are you so sad?"

"My books are useless; I am useless! Woe is me."

Seeing his friend feeling so low, he began to tell him a story.

The Wounded Fly.

There was a fly that became injured in an accident and lost a wing. The fly was so depressed at not being able to fly anymore.

"I am a fly but I cannot fly! I should be called a walk, for walking is all I can do. Oh, woe is me!"

An elephant was nearby and overheard the sorrowful fly so wandered over to him. "Oh dear, oh dear! What have we here? A fly with one wing. Why are you so depressed?"

"I am unable to do what I am called. I can no longer soar into the sky and pester human doings, feed from sweet treats and plants. I have to make do with spoilt fruit and walk everywhere."

"But you are still alive! You still breathe and eat. Things change all the time and so you should embrace this change," said the elephant.

"I want to fly again! I want to be who I'm supposed to be."

"Well, maybe this is what you are supposed to be. After all, you are always you and nobody else can be you. Just be."

"I can't be a bee! For two reasons; one, I am now without two wings, henceforth called a walk, and secondly I don't have the right colouring. You need yellow in you and I have no yellow. I have a slight blue hue, but no yellow, so I can't be a bee!"

The elephant sighed, saying, "No. That's not what I meant; I mean just be, as in just be who you are!"

The fly still had a frown though, as he pondered the elephant's words. The elephant reached his trunk over and gently tapped the fly reassuringly.

"Life still goes on. The worst of things can happen to anyone."

Still the fly was not reassured and sulked. The elephant knocked some fruit down for the fly so he could eat but the fly declined. Then a bird came along and ate the fly!

"Hmmmm, yum yum! That surely was one tasty fly."

The elephant ate the fruit he had felled. "No, it was a tasty walk that you ate."

Confused, the bird flew away.

The elephant moved slowly away, elegantly lumbering over the land and as he did so, he saw a young girl looking about.

"Ah! A lovely elephant! Please can you help me?"

The elephant looked at her wondering why she would possibly want to talk to him.

"I seek the magician that lives nearby. I want to learn his secrets, but I cannot find him."

The elephant knelt down to offer his services and the girl climbed up on his back, then he took her to the magician who lived in the cave near the jungle. After a short while, they arrived. Descending from the elephant, she walked over to the cave and started to call out for the magician.

"Who are you?"

"I am Priya and I want to know your deepest secrets, so I too, can make magic!"

"Oh, my child! What I know is no secret, follow me and I shall explain it to you.

THE MAGICIAN.

The magician led Priya outside the cave and he looked upwards, explaining the source of the magic.

"As you look up, according to the time of day, you will see clouds, the sky, the sun or stars. Our sun forms part of the solar system in our galaxy. Beyond our galaxy you can see the light of other galaxies, stars and star nurseries. You are looking at the past. If you were to view even further, you would see the distant past, back to the point where everything began. So, here you are, standing in this moment, now. The past and distant past is with you, now. The inception of creation is with you in this very moment. All is happening now. The light of distant stars has taken thousands of years, just to get to your eyes. Some of those stars are not even there now, they have passed on, being recycled in the universe. The recycling of stars has meant that all things created, have been born from the stars. Your very self, your blood, your bones, rocks, trees, plants, animals, insects, birds, everything has been created from elements that were once stardust. Creation is still happening, as we look about us. And all this is still happening now, in this moment, as you look up into the heavens. In this moment you are outside of time and the possibilities are endless.

"The gears of time, as we know it, are the earth's passage around the sun; our part of the spiral arm whirling around the galaxy, which itself is moving in the ocean of the universe. And in this moment, anything is possible. As you look at yourself, you are seeing one outcome that the universe discovered by making you. There are countless outcomes, countless choices, all available within this moment. Look about you and see the diversity in plants, animals, colours, shapes, forms, people and places, all created and each a fresh expression of the cosmos.

"Now think about what you are facing in your own life. If you are saying that you think you can't do it, if you think there's no choice, think again. For in this moment, the universe is in and around you, all of time is happening now, here. The future is waiting for you to make a decision. Tonnes of possibilities have enabled you to be here now, and they are endless.

"The magic I have, is the magic of moments, knowing that all possibilities are here, devoid of time, and you are a manifestation of them. Don't ever think that you don't have time, for you do. This moment is eternal. There has only ever been one moment and it is now. The magic is in this moment, where all is one, for all are made from the same elements, the same stardust, all being connected in this simple way. The magic is timeless, bringing the past and future together at the present time, making this moment eternal. And you are here in this eternity, this moment, where the magic resides and pulses through your veins. It's in the very air you breathe. This is creation happening now. As you witness it, it witnesses you. You are the magic happening now and it is in you. Everything is simply being. The magic is within you. The magic is all about you. You are living magic. This is the present, the present moment and it is a gift to you. And this is the magic of moments."

Astounded, Priya considered what she had been told, staring up into the sky. With this secret, she made her way back to her village.

"Here comes the magician!" shouted her father as he saw her coming down the path. "Did you find the magic you were searching for?"

Smiling brightly, she explained what the magician had told her, very excitedly.

"Good, good! I'm so happy you found it. What will you do now, with this knowledge?"

"I will share it with anyone who wants to know about it."

"Good, good!"

So, Priya grew up knowing all about the magic, sharing it with anyone who wanted to know and as she grew, so also did her wisdom. She flourished into a wise woman, entertaining all and any who would talk to her.

Then one day, when Priya was about 23 years old, a man came to her village, looking for the magician. He had travelled far and wide to find him until he happened upon this particular village and began asking for him amongst the villagers, who told him to speak to Priya.

When she saw him, she noticed his dark eyes and that light went into them, but none came out, and she sensed a terrible darkness within them.

"I hear you know of the magician," said Kayden. "May I ask where he is?"

Priya looked him over asking why he wanted to know. Smiling, he replied, "I am Kayden, an old acquaintance of his. I am looking to re-establish our friendship, but no longer know where he lives."

"If you travel through the jungle, pass the Bodhi tree, then head toward the mountain, go by the narrow path and over the stone bridge you will see a cave. He lives within the cave and you will know it's the right one for old drawings will be on the cave walls.

"Jungle, Bodhi tree, mountain, narrow path, stone bridge and cave with old drawings."

"Yes."

"Thank you, young lady, I'm much obliged," smiled Kayden, then set on his way, as he wrapped a linen scarf around his head and put his staff forward to match his first step. Following the advice, he travelled through the jungle until he passed by the Bodhi tree, looked about for a mountain and once he spied it on the horizon, he aimed for it. After a while he came across the narrow path and followed it then passed over a stone bridge and soon was in sight of the cave.

Upon entering, he saw old cave drawings and knew he was in the right place. The cave was deep and becoming dark, for twilight was upon him. Expecting the magician to return soon, he sat down cross legged and awaited. Then he waited some more. And then waited even longer.

As the sun lit up the cave at dawn, Kayden thought he saw the silhouette of a man, but it wasn't, for it was a monkey. He welcomed the monkey and said, "I know you are the magician and I have come for you. I want the power you possess, so that I may have it, then there will be no more need of you and all who seek, shall find only me."

The monkey stood still, then laughed, so Kayden tried to catch the monkey. Eventually, he caught it and bound it tightly, so it could not escape and hurt the monkey hoping it would turn back in to the magician, but this did not work. Then Kayden thought, 'If I release the monkey, it may turn back in to the magician, for it may be unable to change, being bound and tied.' So he released the monkey, but it did not change to become the magician, escaping to the jungle instead. So Kayden sat back down.

A short while later, a large bird flew into the cave. He welcomed the bird and Kayden said, "I know you are the magician and I have come for you. I want the power you possess, so that I may have it, then there will be no more need of you and all who seek, shall find only me." The bird settled, then laughed to the sky, so Kayden tried to catch the bird. Eventually, he caught it and bound it tightly, so it could not escape and hurt the large bird hoping it would turn back in to the magician, but this did not work. Then Kayden thought, 'If I release the bird it may turn back in to the magician, for it may be unable to change, being bound and tied.' So he released the bird, but it did not change to become the magician, escaping instead and it flew away. So Kayden sat back down.

A short while later, a panther entered the cave. He welcomed the panther and Kayden said, "I know you are the magician and I have come for you. I want the power you possess, so that I may have it, then there will be no more need of you and all who seek, shall find only me." The panther sat down, then laughed, so Kayden tried to catch the panther. Eventually, he caught it and bound it tightly, so it could not escape and hurt the panther hoping it would turn back in to the magician, but this did not work. Then Kayden thought, 'If I release the panther it may turn back in to the magician, for it may be unable to change, being bound and tied.' So he released the panther, but it ran away to the jungle.

A short while later, a tiger entered the cave. He welcomed the tiger and Kayden said, "I know you are the magician and I have come for you. I want the power you possess, so that I may have it, then there will be no more need of you and all who seek, shall find only me." The tiger prowled about, then roared so Kayden went to try and capture it. The tiger became very quiet and Kayden neared, getting closer and closer. The tiger sneered, yet Kayden grew closer and closer still. The tiger roared, yet Kayden took himself closer and yet closer still, until only a breath separated them. Kayden looked in to the tiger's big, dark eyes and saw light going to the eyes, but none coming out and sensed a darkness within the beast. Kayden moved in to catch the tiger, moving his hands slowly with the rope so to bind it and as he was about to snare the beast, it placed its large mouth over Kayden's head. Kayden went very, very still. Then the tiger clamped his teeth over the man's head and wragged him about, tossing him all over, like a rag doll. Then Kayden's neck snapped and the tiger stopped, so to eat his body and arms and legs.

A few hours later, the magician arrived at the cave after his long journey, for he had been to visit an old friend. He saw the bones of a man and they were freshly stripped of meat, with a tiger nibbling at the leg of the dead man.

"Oh dear! Oh dear! I think I best move to another cave! This one seems much to dangerous," said the magician.

The tiger turned to him and said, "The cave is not dangerous, but the men who visit here are!"

"Well," said the magician, "thank you for your advice!"

And the tiger replied, "You're most welcome."

So the magician turned and went to find himself another home. Walking along the path, he crossed a stone bridge and then followed a narrow lane. He passed the Bodhi tree then went into the jungle, where he spent the night.

Waking at sunrise, a small bird brought him some fruit which he ate, before setting off for a town, or maybe a village, or maybe a city. The path he took led him to a city this time and it was very large and very grand. Traders and marketers sold rich foods, fine clothes and jewellery of finest Indian gold. He could smell the many scents; jasmine, herbs, flowers, rosewater, freshly cooked spices and vegetables.

"Hey! Hey you!"

A trader shouted as a young boy ran away with some fruit, chasing after him. The magician saw the child running, as well as the trader chasing, so changed his appearance to that of a blind man. He could do so, for after all, he was a magician.

As the trader came closer, the magician moved his staff into the path of the trader, tripping him over.

"What are doing you old fool?"

"I'm ever so sorry, I am blind and could not see you! Forgive me, sir! I humbly apologize."

The trader picked himself up and dusted himself down and muttered under his breath. The magician, however, remained as a blind man and went to find the child who took the fruit. After a short while, he heard a mango being eaten and ventured near to the noise.

"Ah! Is that a nice fresh mango I hear?"

"Yes," said the boy.

"I'll wager that was stolen from the vendor along the street!"

"Well, he has more than enough! And I, we'll, I am an orphan, with no job, no money, no food!"

"Is it right that you should steal though?"

The boy did not answer.

"Uhmm," said the blind man. "No answer does not mean there is no reply! Tell me, have you ever heard of the magic flower?"

"What magic flower?"

"Obviously not then! Well, let me tell you of this wonderful, magic flower...

THE MAGIC FLOWER.

Deep in the jungle, of the northern land, was a lake and in the middle of the lake was a magic flower, which only grew here, and nowhere else. It was beautiful, with rose-gold leaves and a head of sapphires. No one knew of the flower and its location, except for a certain woman, but she kept it a secret. For many years, her family kept knowledge of its location hidden from everyone until one day when the woman knew she was going to die. With her last few breaths, she told her daughter of the magic flower and where it resided.

"There, in the middle of the lake you will find the flower, with leaves of rose-gold and a head of sapphires. You must tell no one of it, keep it a secret for years to come! Then tell only your daughter."

"Yes, Mama," said the daughter, as her mother sadly departed this realm.

Now, a certain young man was nearby, who had just kissed his fiancée goodnight and he happened to overhear what was said through the nearby window. 'If I could give my wife to be this wonderful flower, well, she would love me forever and be awestruck by its beauty,' he thought, so went around to the front of the building to see where the house was. After recognising its location, he left and waited until after the funeral of the woman's mother, then asserted to himself that he would find and have this magic flower.

The funeral passed, and one night when the daughter left the house that was her mother's, he followed her. Under the full moon, she walked for what seemed like forever. The young man was following her, waiting to see if she was going to the lake where the magic flower was. However, she did not. So he went back to his home and waited until the next night, but she did not visit it then either, or the night after that, or even the night after that. Eventually, she did wander off to view the magic flower. Under cover of night, under the moon's bright rays, she visited the lake where the magic flower resided. The sapphire flower glowed brighter than the moon and stars, its rose-gold leaves reflecting the water of the lake. Truly it was a magical sight.

After waiting a short while, the young fiancé moved towards the lake, then making sure the area was clear, he swam the lake to gather the flower for himself. He swam as quietly as he could and eventually came to where the magic flower was. His eyes glowed as his hands gently gathered the majestic plant. Placing it under his tunic, he swam back to the shore, removed himself from the lake and then went home.

At his wedding, he presented his wife with the magic flower for her wedding present from him. She was amazed and aghast at its beauty. Everyone who saw it commented on how wonderful the flower was.

"I also hear that it is magical!" said the groom.

And everyone asked the groom where he acquired it from and in which way it was magical, but he could not answer. All looked at it and marvelled over its exquisite nature. There was one person in particular who saw it and said to their self, "I want that flower!"

Now this person was a lady of refinement, who had only the best clothes, best perfumes, best jewellery and best house. She desired the flower so much that she hired a thief to steal the magic flower from the bride's house. And so the thief stole the flower for the refined lady and sold it to her for a thousand rubies. The lady placed the plant in her living room, proud of her acquisition. She invited people to come and visit, just to show it off. And everyone who saw it said how wonderful it was.

"I also hear that it is magical!" said the refined lady.

And everyone asked the lady where she acquired it from and in which way it was magical, but she could not answer. All looked at it and marvelled over its exquisite nature and there was one person in particular who saw it and said to their self, "I want that flower!"

Now this man had been in a soldier in the war and had killed many men. He thought to himself, " I will steal that flower, even if I have to kill her for it!"

So that night, he returned to the house and broke in. He tried to be very quiet, nearing the jewelled flower. However, he did not realize the neighbour had a dog, which started barking. Disturbed by the noise, the lady came to the room where she kept her treasure and in great alarm at seeing the man, she went to scream, but she did not, for he killed her, then left with the magic flower in his grasp.

At home, the man placed it in his bedroom, on the windowsill so the sapphires could catch the starlight at night. Many came to view the flower and commented on how lucky he was and how magnificent it was.

"I also hear that it is magical!" said the former soldier.

And everyone asked the man where he acquired it from and in which way it was magical, but he could not answer. All looked at it and marvelled over its exquisite nature. There was one person in particular who saw it and said to their self, "I want that flower!"

Now this woman was the queen and she had spied it upon the windowsill above the street one night, as the moon and stars brought it to life. 'I must have it,' she thought and told her husband, the king, about it.

"Of course, my love," said the king and saw to it that the man was tried for some crime, so he could behead him and take his land, home and possessions. And so it was, that the queen acquired the magic flower. Many people from many lands came to visit the palace and proclaimed how wonderful and amazing it was.

"I also hear that it is magical!" said the queen.

And everyone asked the queen where she acquired it from and in which way it was magical, but she could not answer. All looked at it and marvelled over its exquisite nature. There was one person in particular who saw it and said to their self, "I want that flower!"

And this person was a king of another land. So when he returned home to his palace and kingdom, he contrived a reason for war, then he would fight the other king's soldiers, conquer his land and plunder his riches, and the magic flower.

However, on the first day of war, a young woman arrived and asked for the magic flower. The queen asked her what it looked like and the woman described it perfectly.

"I must return it to its home, for the power has become too great to handle! So please, for everyone's sakes, please return it to me!"

"I hear that it is magical," said the queen, "but I have not yet seen its magical properties, even though it is exquisitely beautiful."

"On the contrary, my queen, it has revealed its dark power, thus I must return it to where it lives, far away from the hearts of men and women."

The king agreed and gave the flower back to the young woman, who took it home, walked for what seemed an eternity, then went to the lake, swam out to the middle and placed it back on the lilly-pad, where it resided.

Eventually the years passed by and like her mother, she was about to pass on. She called her eldest daughter to her and told her, with her last few breaths, of the magic flower and where it resided.

"There, in the middle of the lake you will find the flower, with leaves of rose-gold and a head of sapphires. You must tell no one of it, keep it a secret for years to come! Then tell only your daughter."

"Yes, Mama," said the daughter, as her mother made ready to pass over. The daughter begged her mother not to go, but the mother gently assured her daughter by stroking her.

The daughter made arrangements for the funeral with great care, even though her grief seemed almost too great to bare. Other people helped with the necessary tasks, including her uncle, who took time to help console his niece.

"Oh, my child! Do not worry, your mother is now free from suffering. She did not want to leave you; in fact no one wants to leave this realm until they see the next and then they realize that it is the natural course of things."

"What happens, uncle?"

"Ah, let me see... It's like going for a swim.."

THE LAKE.

"When one approaches the stage in this life where they leave for the next, they see the lake. Now, this lake has the most still waters and beautiful flowers resting within it. On the other shore are the ancestors, those of your family that have already swum there and they are there to greet you.

"Once you see your relatives on the other shore, you smile and wave to them, then dip your toes into the crystal waters of the lake and begin to swim, but in this lake, as you swim, you do not need to come up for air. You relax and swim under the water, wondering why you no longer have to breathe. And as you swim,

you see all the colours refracting in the crystal waters; violet, green, blue, red, purple and you are bathed in the wondrous, bright light of the lake.

"Then as you reach the other shore, you ascend out of the waters and walk to be greeted by others who have come here before you. Relations and friends greet you and then you realize, there is no fear, no pain, no suffering, no need and no want. It is peaceful and here you have reached the shore of eternity, the rest from striving for things. This is the journey we all take."

His niece listened in awe of what he was saying. Then he hugged his niece and kissed her forehead. They then went to join the funeral procession. At the site where her mother's mortal body was to be placed to rest and absorbed into the earth, many gathered and the priest began the service.

As the body was committed to the elements, he began reciting a song, "Lead us from ignorance to wisdom, from darkness to light, from death to eternity," then read a passage from a book, about moving through life to death, with everything being provided by a higher power and this intrigued the niece.

After the service, she went up to the priest and asked him questions about the higher power he had talked about.

"Oh, this is an interesting topic! Many have their own understanding of it, but it can generally be seen as 3 opinions. Have you heard of the three birds?"

"No, I have not."

"Well then, let me tell you..."

The Three Birds.

There were three birds sitting in the tree. One was superstitious, another believed in nothing and the other had a spiritual outlook. The superstitious bird said, "If I tap my beak three times on the branch before I fly away, I always find food."

The unbeliever said, "I always find food, no matter how long it takes me."

And the third bird said, "I have faith that I will find food, but then the food finds me!"

"So," asked the niece," people either believe, don't believe, or are superstitious? "

"It's one way of understanding it. Many people believe many things. Some say that there is a force which we call upon, and most call this, 'God,' whereas others some believe in the attributes of the force as many, 'gods.' Some just merely refer to it as the universe and then there are those who just don't believe. Those who don't believe but practice rituals before doing something, well, they're the superstitious ones. It is up to you to discover what you do, or don't, believe."

"And what do you believe?"

"Ah, well, I'm biased as I am a priest within my faith! So I can give my opinion based on what I think, but you should form your own understanding. Read. Speak to others from other faiths and those who don't believe. Make your own mind up! And let no one make it for you!"

The niece stopped and thought for a moment, then asked, "What is faith?"

The priest laughed and said, "Have you heard the tale about the cows?"

The niece shook her head, so the priest guided her to a shady spot in the afternoon sun and they sat down.

THE COWS.

Somewhere in a field, some place, some time ago, there was a cow just chewing the grass and masticating. As it ruminated, it thought to itself, "It's getting ever so dry these days! We need some rain, otherwise the grass will wither and dry out, and then I'll have nothing to eat!"

The cow thought about it some more and then decided to talk to the sky and said, "I don't know if anyone, or anything, is up there, but I know that rain comes downwards from where you are. Would you, whatever you are, be so kind as to send some rain please?"

After a short while, there was no answer, but a little shower of rain fell from a light grey cloud.

"Oh! Thank very much!"

The next day, the cow was thinking to itself again about the grass and rain once more.

"Hmm, I think we need a little more rain," said the cow, then turned to the sky and said, "I don't know if anyone, or anything, is up there, but I know that rain comes downwards from where you are. Would you, whatever you are, be so kind as to send some rain please?"

And sure enough, a little later, some more rain fell, pleasing the cow. It was overjoyed and started jumping about and mooing gratefully.

"What on earth are you doing?" asked another cow.

"It rained! It rained!"

"You silly cow! Of course it rained! Why wouldn't it?"

"Ah, but I asked for it to happen!"

"Don't be daft! Who did you ask? Another cow?"

"No, I asked whatever is up there to send some down here, and they did!"

The second cow was not convinced and raised its eyebrows.

"So you spoke to this invisible thing and it answered you?"

"Well, it didn't speak, but it sent rain!"

"Prove it..."

"Okay. If you agree, with what I say now, please say, 'I agree' after my request...."

"Okay, okay!"

"I don't know if anyone, or anything, is up there, but I know that rain comes downwards from where you are. Would you, whatever you are, be so kind as to send some rain please?"

"I agree."

Suddenly, a heavy shower descended from the sky, drenching the two cows with refreshing rain. Both of them started jumping about and mooing loudly with gratitude. So much so that a third cow noticed them and looked over with curiosity.

"Oi! What on earth are you doing?"

"It rained! It rained!"

"You silly cows! Of course it rained! Why wouldn't it?"

"Ah, but we asked for it to happen!"

"Don't be daft! Who did you ask? This other cow?"

"No, we asked whatever is up there to send some down here, and they did!"

The third cow was not convinced and raised its eyebrows.

"So you two spoke to this invisible thing and it answered you?"

"Well, it didn't speak, but it sent rain!"

"Prove it..."

"Okay. If you agree, with what we say now, please say, 'I agree' after my request...."

"Alright. Go on then, this'll be good! (You daft cows!)"

"Right then. We don't know if anyone, or anything, is up there, but we know that rain comes downwards from where you are. Would you, whatever you are, be so kind as to send some rain please?"

Then sure enough, a few moments later, it started raining with a heavy downpour, dowsing the three cows until they were drenched. Even though very wet, all 3 cows danced and mooed with joy.

In the field next to theirs, stood a bull, all by itself. It had been watching them all the time.

"How did you do that?"

The first cow, excitedly said, "We've been asking for rain, and it worked!!!"

"More like a coincidence if you ask me! I have been watching you dippy cows all the time and each time, I saw grey clouds coming across the sky."

"That's because we asked for them!"

"Who did you ask?"

"Er, well, I don't know who or what, but it answered! Didn't i? You saw it didn't you? And you! All 3 of us witnessed it."

"So this 'thing,' that you don't know about, which you can't see and who doesn't speak back to you...."

"The one whom we call upon..."

"Yeah, this 'thing,' what else can they do? Send a tornado of dung? Throw cowpats at you with the wind?"

The three cows looked at each other with confused looks on their faces.

"Er, well, we don't know!"

"Alright then. I've got something to ask for; I'd like a nice, big, gnarly tree so I can scratch myself on it. And I want to hear some thunder in the sky, so it breaks up this humidity, 'coz it's just so warm."

The cow tilted it's head from side to side, weighing up the request.

"Er, I'll give it a try! I haven't asked for anything like that yet... So bear with me...."

"Here we go," said the bull, starting to laugh at the cow. "Making excuses before it doesn't happen, are we?"

"No! But I'm sure there's something up there!"

"Yeah, yeah.... Come on; big scratchy tree and thunder, if you please!"

"Well, it's not up to me is it?"

"No, it's up to the one we're calling upon," said another cow. The bull began mocking and shaking his head in disbelief. Then the cows made the request.

"We don't know your name, or where you are exactly, but we know that rain comes downwards from where you are. Would you, whatever you are, be so kind as to send this bull a big, gnarly tree so he can scratch his self on it and some thunder in the sky, so it breaks up this humidity, er, p-per-please?"

In an instant, a clap of thunder was heard directly above them, after a shocking bolt of lightning struck the ground nearby. It was raining again and the cows could feel the humidity clearing. They then looked around for a tree, to see if that request had been answered, but saw no rough, gnarly tree in the neighbouring field. What they did see though, was steam arising from a certain point in the field next to them. Looking over the fence, one of the cows saw something interesting.

"Anyone of us order steak?"

"No," said the other cow and another commented, "Definitely not!"

"Ah... Well, I think I know what's happened to the bull..."

"Where's the tree?" asked the third cow.

"Well, there's no need for it now, really, if you care to take a look..."

And they chuckled, then thanked the one they called upon, for the fresh rain and mooed loudly with gratitude, as they jumped and danced around the field.

The priest smiled as he finished reciting the tale and heard the young lady chuckle.

"So that is faith; believing that something will happen, or believing that some higher power will make it happen!"

The woman smiled with comprehension at the priest's tale, whilst considering other questions, but the priest made his excuses and went on his way into the nearby town.

As he travelled, the birds began their evensong and swifts swooped low. He saw the town in the near distance and the sun painting the sky with pastel shades. As he neared, a tatty, raggy man approached. As they were about to pass each other, the shoddily dressed man asked a favour.

"Excuse me, kind sir! I see you are a man of faith. Could you possibly lend me a courtesy, say of a few coins for a drink and maybe some bread. I am good for it, having a small wage at my home, over the hill and next village. You can trust me to return the funds, or maybe a favour instead...."

The priest looked him over.

"Why should I not trust you?' Is a question that I did not consider until you mentioned it. Here, have these coins and if the weather breaks, or we meet again, you may repay me, but I'll hold you to no promise. Here."

The man took the coins and smiled with glee.

"Oh, thank you kind sir! You're a credit to your faith in your fellow man and whatever else you, you subscribe to. A true, kind person."

"Thank you! You're welcome."

"As for the trust, you say you require no promise, but let me give you a story, a parable if you like, that one such as yourself might use for a cautionary tale, lecture, or sermon."

The priest saw the last of the sun dipping behind the horizon.

"Go on then, for such anecdotes do have good use in my line of work."

So the tramp-like looking man beckoned him to sit with him on the roadside and then he relayed the story...

THE BALD MAN.

In the town, that's just over there, by that wotsit and near to the thing, no not that one, the thing next to it, there is a barbershop. Now inside the shop lives an extraordinary barber, who has been profoundly blind since his birth. His skill has been to assess a head by touch alone and they say, that's them, not I, they say that he is deft with the scissor and also with the blade.

One day, a stranger happened to stumble into the town, that one just over there, by the doodah and next to the thing, no not that one, but the thing next to it, and the stranger was bald. Well, almost, but not quite yer know, just a bit of fluff growing over ear and off the crown. He was almost completely bald, but not fully, nor profoundly bald, if you catch my drift. Well, this stranger was a little tired and weary, not a lot, just a bit, yer know, like when one's just finished work, or finished a labour. A tad tired he was and went to the saloon, to refresh his gullet; not to get drunk, that was never in his thought, but possibly in mind. So he wanders deliberately into the saloon and stumbles upon a licensed bar. 'What fortune,' he thinks and orders a drink, not a large one, nor a small one, just one big and wet enough to moisten his throat and stomach.

"Hello, barkeep," says the fellow, "may I possibly have a drink please that's large enough to moisten my mouth but not small enough to make me thirst for more? Just one large enough, not too big, nor too small."

"How about a whisky," asks the barkeep.

"Ah, sir, you know your trade. The bottle will do, so I can measure the quantity just right, so it's not too small, nor too big, if you get my drift..."

And the barkeep passes him over a bottle of finest whisky and a glass without a handle that's a little bit small, but not too large neither. And the baldish man pours a drink, just the right size, for he is, at the moment, of sound mind and can gauge the correct amount of alcohol required to quench his thirst. Then, the bald fellow catches his handsome reflection in the mirror behind the bar, 'neath the shelves and above the cupboard.

"My, my, I am handsome! What could enhance my roguish looks? I know, a haircut is what I need! For a haircut is a hair enhanced! Barkeep, whither is thy barber, or dentist, that I may approach him and barter for a shave?"

"See Blind Jim, across the street, he's the one we all use."

"Blind Jim? That inspires no confidence! I see cigarette paper over your neck and cheeks, where a follicle's been nipped, I fancy."

"I shaved myself this morning, that's why I'm blooded, but we all use Blind Jim for the dentist and barber."

"Well, after my instinct I must go but first have some courage, save I face my fate in the hands of a blind barber who shaves sighted men and has a beard of his own. Why does he not shave himself?"

"On account of his facial balance. He too is bald, but as a coot, and without the beard, he's all too weird, looking that is."

"Hmmm," thinks the bald, but not profoundly bald man. "Then in him I place my trust! And I trust his razor has no rust? For he can't see blemish, blade or pimple!"

"His wife changes the blade each day! Are you going over or what?"

"After another spoonful of luck, or courage, whatever favours me most."

The man slid the glass over the polished bar to the barkeep who wasn't too far away. Taking another swig of his concentrated ale, the almost bald man went to meet the blade. And over he went, to see Blind Jim. He crosses the street, up on to the path, looks in the window to see the lay of the land, catches his ruggedly handsome reflection in the window, then goes in as so to enhance his visage for self and the women.

"Hello," he says," are you Blind Jim?"

"Well, yes that I am, come right on in!"

So the man sits down in the chair, bottle in hand and about to put his trust in a blind man.

"I've come for a shave, on my head and round to the chin, for I'm almost bald, as a coot. I have this little bit of fluff on top and around the ears, not too much, but more than a little. I need the skills of a barber to smooth my head and face, can you help?"

"Well, I surely can! Sit down and I'll come over to assist."

"Now that doesn't inspire the confidence, as I'm already seated! Why should I trust my head and face to a stranger, who's been blind since birth?"

"Sir, I'll have you know that many a folk have commented on my certain skill to wend a razor over scalp and chin! I got myself a bonafide certification from the barber's academy at St Louis!"

"It's bonafide? How much it cost you?"

"Sir, I paid not a dime! That was earned by blood, sweat and tears!"

"Whose blood? Why did they sweat? And of whom was the tears? The widows of the many men you slain whilst earning a trade?"

"I'll have you know I'm bonafide! I've shaved for nigh on the best of 30 years!"

"30 years? So you're senile as well as blind? Heck, I must be outta my mind!"

"Sir, you'll just have to trust my skill with the blade, for I never lost a customer, or cent, to my trade! Trust me, I'm bonafide. Now let's take a look at your scalp..."

And the blind Jim placed his hands over the gentleman's head, gently feeling with fingertip and palm, then without delay began to mix soap with oil of the palm, until the paste was frothy and thick. A brush was then placed in the bowl and the brush was rubbed with lather into the near profoundly bald man's head. There was not too much, nor too little and none was needed for the crown in the middle of his head. Then dawned the moment of dread, for the blade was sharpened on the strop, ready to slice follicle from head.

"Sir, if you're ready, I'll begin..."

"I'll never be ready, but go ahead and start! And be careful not to shed my blood, it belongs to my heart! And keep my head attached to my neck, it's been that way since I was born and I'd like to keep it there!"

"Sir, have a little faith in my skill. Everyone in this town trusts me to cut their hair and shave their skin."

"What everyone? Even the women?"

"No, no, no! Just the men! No clam up, calm down and let me begin."

So the blade neared his flesh and moment he'd dreaded came to bare. The first run of the blade was smooth and when he dared to open an eye, and sneak a look, the mirror showed no trace of red. There was no blood, just bare skin instead. Another run of the blade completed real soon and he snuck another look and still no crimson was on his head. So he opened his eyes wide and observed the man who was truly bonafide, with certification from St Louis, as he shaved round lips and neck, ear and eyelid, for oh yes, the barber he also shaved the brows off of eyes with a flick of the wrist, being so adept was he with the blade, the now profoundly bald man had indeed no need to have feared or be in mortal dread. And after Blind Jim had completed, he rubbed oil over the man's head. The stranger waited until the towel was removed, then inspected the mirror to confirm the truth.

"You sir, are truly bonafide! And with your skill, you should have such pride! You sir, have made me as smooth and soft as the day my mama nursed me at her breast!"

"Of course I have! I may be blind, but I ain't ignorant. I have used hands all my life and the one thing I know, is how to feel to get ahead!"

"Why, I certainly mostly apologize for any inference that I trusted you not! You sir, are a barbershop genius!"

"See, I told you I was bonafide!"

"You truly did. My faith and trust has been rectified. I'm sorry for not placing my trust in you and making myself out to be a fool."

"Aww, have no worry, your fear was justified, just as it was when I was in training, for many young men feared for their lives... But least said the better there as it does not inspire the best of confidence and if I'd led with that particular argument, well, let's just say it would have seen you scruffier tomorrow than the day before yesterday!"

Then the stranger paid his fare, whilst feeling his smooth head that was now fluff free and bare.

The Wedding Cake.

"And that is the tale of the blind man, my friend."

The priest laughed heartily at the parable, commenting that it was truly inspired.

"Tell me, do you have any more stories such as just recited?"

"Alas, no, I have not 2 or 3, just the one."

"Well, I very much enjoyed it. Now you take care, for I must make my way over to that town."

So the men parted ways and the priest went over to the town whilst the raggy man went to the nearby village.

As the tramp entered the town, a warden approached him and arrested him.

"We have no vagrants in this town! Be gone or I shall chain you in a cell over night!'

"But, sir, I am no vagrant! My appearance misleads you! I know the priest of these parts and know him well I do. Not too much to be over familiar, but enough to be a friend and not an acquaintance. He can vouch for me..."

"Well, he is not here to vouch for you! He has gone to another house of prayer tonight."

"What misfortune I have! First you think I am a vagrant, then the one man who can verify my, my.. er, wealth, is not here? What grave misfortune! Well, you shall have to lock me up overnight in the cell, save risking your character and people thinking I'm a vagrant, a tramp, a hobo..... Please think of me and moreover, of your own good standing...."

The warden considered what had been said, then with sound judgement, led the man to the cell. Locking him in, he left the man unchained, with a pitcher of beer and a large chunk of bread with some cheese.

"Ah, sir! You are most kind. I won't hear a bad word said about you!"

"Bad word? What bad word?"

"Well, they..."

"Who?"

"Them, those who say, 'He never caught those who ate the wedding cake?'"

"Cake? What wedding cake?'

"Ah, I see...."

"See what? What wedding cake?"

"You don't know about the wedding cake?"

Appearing dumbfounded, the warden stopped short.

"Er, oh! That wedding cake!"

"Which wedding cake?"

"That one, y'know.... I'm currently investigating at the moment y'know..."

"Ah! Right! Well who did it?"

"Er, well it's still under investigation, y'see..."

"Well, maybe I can help, for I am a witness to what occurred."

"You saw who ate it?"

"I saw many eat it!"

"Many? Many? How many?"

"I shall tell you. If you agree to tell no one it was I who told you, I will tell you. But if you do tell that I told you, then I shall deny ever talking to you, as if I never, ever telled anyone! So I'll only tell, if you never tell that I told you, you agree?"

The confused warden was flummoxed but anxiously said, "Come on then, tell me!"

"Well," began the vagrant, "there was this wedding, just the other day. Not yesterday, nor yesterday's yesterday, or yesterday's yesterday yesterday, if you catch my drift, but it wasn't yesteryear neither. However, it was more than a few yesterdays, but not nearly a month of yesterdays..."

"Yes, yes..."

"Well the bride had ordered the most biggest-est cake to show off her marriage to all the guests. However, the cake was so big, that a box could not house it! It wasn't huge, but wasn't little, but bigger than a box but not as small as a thistle, it was just so high, if you catch my meaning?"

"Yes..."

"So the cake deliverer delivered it into an adjoining room, not the adjoining room but the room next to it, but not next to the loo, the room that is next to the other one, yer know the one?"

"Er, yes, yes, get on with it....'

"And this room, the one that is not the adjoining room but the room next to it, but not next to the loo, the room that is next to the other one, that of which you know I'm talking of..."

"Yes, yes....."

"Well this room, it had door, that wasn't ajar, but neither closed as in locked, for this door had a lock but no key, a key somewhere but not there, neither here, nor not over there, this key is currently without it's lock, but closed enough to contain the cake.

"Now, everyone, who was anyone, knew of the grandeur of the cake, for they'd heard the cake baker brag about the size of the cake they had baked and make no mistake, they'd prouded themselves on the large cake they'd ever baked making sundry and all aware of the magnificence of the cake. And maybe it was this that caused the misfortune that was cast upon the enormous baked cake they had maked. However, I digress, for what happened was this: a guest, the first to arrive, snook about the place with curious interest, and lo, behold, it founded the cake! They ventured into the room, the one that is not the adjoining room but the room next to it, but not next to the loo, the room that is next to the other one, that of which you know I'm talking of, and opened the door, that wasn't ajar, but neither closed as in locked, for this door had a lock but no key, if you remember, a key that's somewhere but not there, neither here, nor not over there, the key that's currently without it's lock, but closed enough to contain the cake; well, they went into the room and said, 'My, my! What an enormous cake! It looks so beautiful and tasty. I wonder how long it would take to bake this cake? I wonder if, if I just had a nibble, so taste, just a little, not a lot, not too small, neither big, just enough to have a morsel and taste this magnificent cake....' And so they did, and then they slid out from the room and met the bride and groom.

"And guests by now were arrived, coming to visit from far and wide, and they started snooping about, as people do; not all, but some, you know, just a few. and lo, behold, another founded the cake! They ventured into the room, the one that is not the adjoining room but the room next to it, but not next to the loo, the room that is next to the other one, that of which you know I'm talking of, and

opened the door, that wasn't ajar, but neither closed as in locked, for this door had a lock but no key, if you remember, a key that's somewhere but not there, neither here, nor not over there, the key that's currently without it's lock, but closed enough to contain the cake; well, they went into the room and said, 'My, my! What an gigantic cake! It looks so beautiful and tasty. I wonder how long it would take to bake this cake? I wonder if, if I just had a nibble, so taste, just a little, not a lot, not too small, neither big, just enough to have a morsel and taste this magnificent cake....' And thus, they did, then out of the room they slid to go congratulate the bride and groom.

"And then what happened? Another guest started mooching about, as people do; not all, but some, you know, just a few. and lo, behold, another founded the cake! They ventured into the room, the one that is not the adjoining room but the room next to it, but not next to the loo, the room that is next to the other one, that of which you know I'm talking of, and opened the door, that wasn't ajar, but neither closed as in locked, for this door had a lock but no key, if you remember, a key that's somewhere but not there, neither here, nor not over there, the key that's currently without it's lock, but closed enough to contain the cake; well, they went into the room and said, 'My, my! What a humongous cake! It looks so beautiful and tasty. I wonder how long it would take to bake this cake? I wonder if, if I just had a nibble, so taste, just a little, not a lot, not too small, neither big, just enough to have a morsel and taste this magnificent cake....' And thus, they did, then out of the room they slid to go congratulate the bride and groom.

'And as the wedding breakfast continued, many more slipped through the door, and what's more, all who entered, though not all together, but individually, at one time or another, all said, 'My, my! What a simply huge cake! It looks so beautiful and tasty. I wonder how long it would take to bake this cake? I wonder if, if I just had a nibble, so taste, just a little, not a lot, not too small, neither big, just enough to have a morsel and taste this magnificent cake....' And thus, they did, then out of the room they slid to go congratulate the bride and groom. And all the guests did this.

"Then the time came, to unveil the cake and it was brought from the room, the one that is not the adjoining room but the room next to it, but not next to the loo, the room that is next to the other one, that of which you know I'm talking of, and placed in the centre of the banquet room, for all to see, with a sheet on top, for the sake of formality. Then the toastmaster gathered sundry and all together, for the grand unveiling of the most grandest-est cake a Baker ever baked.

"The room was silenced by the tinkling of spoon against a glass, for the moment had now come at last, to reveal the cake in all its glory, and can you guess what happens next in my story?

"The toastmaster lifted the sheet aloft, and all the guests gasped, paused in a deathly silence, which after a moment was broken by a solitary cough. 'What's happened here? Where is my cake?' asked the bride. To which everyone, in unison replied, 'It was not I!'

"The groom then raised an eyebrow and said, 'That's not the question; you've answered another instead! But now we know who ate the cake; you've all confessed!' And the bride was mighty sore and harsh words were said, until the minister in charge, encouraged forgiveness instead. To this note, bride and groom gave forgiveness and that, sir, is who committed the crime, as God is my witness."

After hearing the prisoner, the warden wondered what to do. Surely there had been a crime, but whom should he arrest?

"Shall I arrest everyone, or just one, then? Maybe the first guest..."

"Or maybe arrest none! For forgiveness was granted upon them by the bride and priest. Should you arrest someone who has been graciously pardoned? Wouldn't that be a crime in itself?"

The warden thought about it, long and hard.

"One supposes that I should do nowt! And that I assuredly will do, since they have been forgiven."

Now that it was settled in his mind, he went to the chair behind his desk, sat himself down and placed his feet on the table. Tilting his hat forward, so to cover his eyes, he made ready for sleep. The vagrant also settled himself down for the night, glad of a roof over his crafty head, as well as some drink, bread and cheese.

The dawn ushered birds to sing and move, doing the things that birds do, which in turn awoke the warden who then made some morning tea. By clinking and cluttering the tin and copper instruments, he awoke the vagrant within the cell.

"Good morning kind sir! Could I be so bold as to ask for a cup of your tea, please? Not a big one, nor little, just the right size to whet my whistle?"

"Aye, you may," said the warden, who did so with haste.

"Ah, you are so very kind."

Now, this morning saw the possibility of the vagrant being released with no place to go, thus a plan was needed to be devised, so he could not be seen to be whom he was, a vagrant, for he'd assured the warden that he wasn't, hadn't he. So the cogs and wheels of his mind turned.

"Tell me, good sir, where is the monastery near here, for I need to visit them on behalf of the priest. He gave me a message for them."

"What message? I'll take it for you..."

"Oh, er, you're too kind, but the message I have has been entrusted to me to deliver specifically, to the one who is specified and if another delivered the specific specificity, a worry would loom in that person's mind. Therefore, if you could guide me to their sanctuary, I'd be most grateful..."

"Show me the message," asked the warden.

"Ah, now it's only in my mind. It was in case anyone else minded what was on the priest's mind, so it was specifically specified to go to this person's mind and no other mind, save the minding of the message fall into the wrong person's mind. If you catch my drift."

The warden thought long and hard, for he was due to release the suspected vagrant this morning anyway.

"Who is it that you need to speak to?"

"Yes, that's right."

"It was a question with choice, not a yes or no to be uttered! So tell me, who is it that you must speak with?"

"Once again, that's correct."

"No, no. Who is needed to receive the message?"

"Once more, that's right."

"Are you trying to deliberately antagonize?"

"No, but Hu is the recipient of the message in my mind."

"Who?"

"Yes, that's true, it is Hu."

"Who IS IT?"

"YES, IT'S HU! For Hu is his name, I'm not making of you a fool. His name is Hu."

"I see... Well, I know not of whom you speak. I can't recall a Hu..."

The vagrant flitted about his eyes, looking to come up with a quick reply.

"Why surely you know Hu! He's the one with the bald head, and a long, but not too long, but not too short whitish beard, that's more grey in it than white; a tall gentle man, whose head touches the sky. He has a scar on his left hand, (or maybe his right) and he talks with a limp, walks with a stutter."

"I cannot recall ever meeting him..."

"You must know him! You know, the one with the bald head, and a long, but not too long, but not too short whitish beard, that's more grey in it than white; a tall gentle man, whose head touches the sky. He has a scar on his left hand, (or maybe his right) and he talks with a limp, walks with a stutter. Carries a leather satchel, for his tin bowl, begs for food at the mill pond, a place of which he is particularly fond."

"The mill pond, you say? I may recall some brother there..."

"Of course you do! You know Hu! Nice bloke, a very kindly man with a cheery disposition, you know who I mean, don't you? Everyone knows him! Anyone who knows who's who knows Hu, save only a tiny few, of whom you might be one, from what I can discern. Fancy not knowing Hu! Sundry and all know good old Hu, he's well known to the most, not so to maybe a few, of whom you might be one, from what I can discern."

Sick of hearing the vagrant going on about the man, the warden wanted rid of him, not being able to listen to him whittle on and on.

"Alright, alright! I'll release you! Go and see this Hu and give him the message you promised to deliver."

"Oh, thank you, thank you. You're very kind. I must, must deliver the message that's in my mind specifically for him."

"Away with you! I cannot stand anymore of your chatter!"

And with that, the vagrant was released, with directions on how to get to the monastery.

"So go to the top of the road, climb the hill, descend the other side, then turn right at river and follow it till you see the monastery."

So the hobo left the cell in the village and began walking to the monastery, having convinced even himself of the mission. He walked to the top of the long village road, climbed over the small hill and headed for the river. Following it along to the east, he eventually arrived at the monastery.

"Is Hu here?"

"Who?"

"That's right."

"Who do you want?"

"Yes, he's the one!"

"Ah, you mean Hu!"

"Yes, Hu is who I mean!"

"Come in and we shall find him," said the monk who answered the bell. The vagrant was shocked that there actually was a monk called, Hu! It amazed him to know that he knew who's who. What a guess! He confessed to himself that it was a narrow escape and startling coincidence.

Two Monks.

After a short while, the monk found Hu, sitting in the gardens. He introduced the vagrant to Hu then left them to talk about whatever they needed to talk about.

Hu was sitting quietly in the garden, beside a fig tree. The large leaves of the tree gently moved in the breeze, fanning him, whilst the shade cooled the warm sun on his head. The vagrant silently sat down and joined him.

"Hello!"

"Good day to you,' said Hu. "And what is your name?"

"A name? Well I never thought of a name!"

"Everybody is somebody until they have no body."

"That is a very good point. It's been many years since I heard my name and I have forgotten it."

"Why has nobody called you by name?"

"I am homeless, that is I am without home and just travel from there to here, maybe over there a bit as well."

"You were born with a name, were you not?"

"Born, yes. With a name? Most probably. Was I not? I would never know. Why?"

"Uhmm, then I shall call you, Wai."

"Why?"

"Well, why not?"

"It is as good a name as any I s'pose!"

"Then Wai it is. Would you join me here? For you would appear to be in need of a roof."

"Why not! "

So the vagrant was named and sat down next to Hu. Time ticked by and Hu said nothing since the welcoming conversation, merely smiling and sitting quietly under the tree.

The stillness was very becoming for the monk, but for the vagrant it was not and he became restless.

"What are we doing then?"

"Something and nothing."

"Is there nothing to do?"

"Yes. Sit and just be. That is the thing that we are doing," said Hu.

"I was hoping for a little conversation, not a long one, nor a short one, but a conversation nevertheless."

"About what?"

"Well, I wouldn't know, not that I should know, but now I know not what to talk about."

"Then why talk if there's nothing to say?"

"Good point!"

"Let us sit and think of what not to say. If you are to stay here, this you must practice!"

So they continued to both sit in silence.

A large sundial lay in the garden, slightly obscured by the tree. A short time passed by and Wai tried to look at the sundial, but couldn't be bothered to move, so asked Hu, "What's the time?"

"Now," was the answer. He was not abrupt, nor rude, just answering gently.

Yet more time passed and Hu was still enjoying the sun, whilst contemplating not thinking.

"What are you thinking about?"

"Oh, nothing," said Hu. "Are you thinking what I'm not thinking?"

"I don't know. What are you not thinking about?"

"Nothing."

"How can you not be thinking about nothing?"

"I never really thought about it!"

"Hmmm....."

More time passed and the restless Wai, fidgeted around trying to view the sundial again.

"What's the time?" asked Wai.

"Now," said Hu

"You said that half an hour ago."

"That was then, this is now."

The two of them then returned to silence.

"Why don't you talk much? You're very hard to make conversation with, you know."

"Before I say anything I ask myself, 'Is it necessary?' Then I think, 'Is it useful?' Then, 'Is it true?' Then finally I ask, 'Is it kind?' And if what I say is necessary, useful, true and kind, I then I say it. If not, then I do not."

Hu then said no more and returned to the silence. After a good while Wai became restless once more.

"What's the time now, Hu?"

"Right now? It's now."

"That's twice in the last hour, you've said that!"

"Well it is now."

"What was it before then?"

"Before this, it was then and before that it just was."

"Was what?"

"Now."

"But how can that be? You said now IS now!" Wai shouted, becoming frustrated by his companion.

"Oh, not anymore it's not."

"What time is it now then?"

"Now."

"You are infuriating!"

"Am I now?"

"Yes!"

"Good. Then you agree I am now."

"I give up!"

"You give up now?"

"Yes!"

"That's your trouble; too much time on your hands," said Hu. "Anyway, why do you ask a question that you know the answer to? You ask the time but are measuring the passing of it."

"Just trying to make conversation, that's all."

"Oh, right."

"Have you ever wondered what this is all about?" asked the vagrant.

"No, I don't," replied Hu.

"I mean, you must think about why are we here and what's the point to existence? Surely!"

"Nah, not really."

"What, never?"

"No."

"How's that?"

"Well, think about this: does a mountain wonder why it was forced out of the sea? Does a feather on a chicken, know it's a chicken feather? Does a leaf on a tree know it's a leaf, or does it think it's just part of the tree? And does an ant think, 'Am I just an ant?'"

"Those are some great questions! But what about the meaning of life? And why are we here? What's the point in all of this?"

"Well, it just is, isn't it. I don't think about it."

"Why?"

"Do you like soya beans?"

The change in conversation perplexed Wai and he pulled a look on his face that was both confused and stumped for an answer.

"Er, I suppose so. What's that got to do with anything?"

"Well, have you consciously thought about if you actually like soya beans?"

"Er, I suppose not!"

"Well, when you have an answer I'll give you my answer."

The quizzical Wai seemed perplexed and didn't know what to say. Hurriedly, he said, "I actually don't like soya beans! Now give me your answer!"

"Fair enough. Now as for the meaning of life, existence and all that stuff, well, I don't know, I don't think about it!"

"Hang on... You said you'd give me an answer!"

"I did. It's just that it's not the one you wanted."

"What? But I asked you why you don't think about these profound questions! So tell me!"

"Soya beans."

"What do you mean, 'soya beans? The reason for existence, life and why we are here is soya beans?"

"For the bean, the whole point of everything is just to grow, exist and be here and eventually be eaten."

"The meaning is just to exist and be consumed?"

"You obviously seem too consumed by these questions....."

"But they're important!"

"To you, maybe. I'm just happy being here now, and to me, that's more important. Oh, and eating soya beans."

Then Wai took himself away, feeling angry and unsatisfied, whilst the soya bean philosopher smiled happily and said to himself, "Maybe I should have told him about bamboo shoots instead...."

When the bell rang out for the evening meal, Hu ventured to the refectory and sat with the others to enjoy their lentils and bread. They all sat with heads bowed until the Abbot had finished offering thanks, then began to eat. After the silence of the meal, they moved to the chapel to observe the evening service, where the Abbott began teaching through his sermon. The lesson this time was about patience and being able to wait, patiently.

"Brothers and sisters, we must remember not only to be patient in waiting for things," said the Abbot, "but be patient with others. Let us recall the command to treat one another in the way we would expect to be treated ourselves. There is a parable which I would like to share with you to demonstrate this.

"A long time ago, deep in the forest, lived a monkey who waited under an apple tree...

The Monkeys.

Above the monkey, on the tree, was an apple waiting to fall. It was out on a limb, of a branch, on the tree. It had been ripening in the sun, waiting to fall and the monkey underneath awaited it to descend to the floor. A chimp came along and saw the monkey staring up at the apple, wondering why he did not simply climb the tree to fetch the apple.

"What are you doing?" asked the chimp.

"Waiting for that apple to fall."

"Why wait? Just climb up and grab the fruit!"

"No, I'm happy just to wait. At the right time, it will fall, then I shall eat it."

"That will take forever! Just grab the apple! Do you want me to get if for you? Is it too high up for you? Are you scared of heights?"

"No," said the monkey, "I'm not scared of heights. I'm happy to wait patiently. In its own good time it will fall and that will be the right time."

"Well, I'm hungry, so if you don't go and grab it, I will!"

"I wouldn't if I were you. See there? There is another tree with fruit on which you can eat from."

The chimp looked about seeing the other tree, then turned back to see the large juicy apple high up in the tree.

"Nah, I want that apple. Last chance mate, get the apple yourself or I will."

"No, I'll wait."

"Right then, that apple is mine..."

So the chimp climbed up the tree and began to tease the monkey as it neared the apple.

"I wouldn't do that, if I was you," shouted the monkey, but the chimp would have none of it and continued to the apple. And as it neared the apple that was on the limb of the branch, that was on the tree, the monkey covered his eyes so he couldn't see, for what was about to happen would be a calamity. The chimp moved from the tree trunk to the limb, then moved slowly towards the branch. As it edged nearer, the branch began to bend. Moving nearer to the apple, the branch bended even more. Then as the chimp became so close to the apple, it bent and bended some more, until it snapped and chimp, branch and apple all fell to the floor.

The monkey moved over to where they all lay and took the apple and began to eat it.

"Yum yum, what a delicious apple! It was definitely worth the wait."

The chimp rubbed his saw head and watched the monkey eat the apple.

"Why didn't you tell me the branch was brittle and about to snap?"

"Well, I did say that you shouldn't do that! And my wait paid off, for eventually the apple fell to me, you see! So it pays to have patience."

The chimp was miffed about the incident and went away sulking, forgetting about the fruit in the other tree. In the distance, he could see a gorilla eating something and decided to move closer, very quietly, so he might see what the gorilla was eating. It was lots of fruit. The chimp excitedly and quietly climbed up a tree to view the banquet of fruit which the gorilla had by its feet. There were mangoes and pears, bananas, oranges, plums, berries and so much more. The chimp thought to himself, "If only I could pinch some of that fruit..." and began devising a plan.

A knock of wood on wood broke the gorilla's concentration and it narrowed its eyes to spy where the sound came from. Then the knock happened again. Then again and again. Being an inquisitive fellow, the gorilla decided to find out what was going on and moved to where he thought he heard the noise. As the gorilla moved away, the chimp quietly moved to where the gorilla had sat and saw all the beautiful, rich, ripe fruit. There was so much, so the chimp decided to take sum. Chuckling to himself, the chimp was so happy to have the fruit, carrying it away to hide and eat it.

As the gorilla returned, he noticed that some of his fruit had gone and he became angry.

"Who has taken my fruit!?" shouted the gorilla, as he stormed about. Continuing to shout, he threw up dead branches and tore up plants. All the while, the chimp chuckled with a mischievous grin, whilst eating the fruit he had stolen.

Soon all the fruit was gone. Night fell, dawn arose and hunger returned to the chimp, so he went hunting for food. There was plenty of fruit in the trees, but as you probably guessed, this is a lazy chimp and he wants everyone to do the work for him, for he just likes to eat the food and not find it. Off he went to find berries and fruit. However, this time, there was no bounty about that another animal had gathered. Thus, he resolved that he must gather the food himself, so he climbed up a tree and started knocking fruit off and pulling berries from plants, letting them fall to the floor and gather, for him to eat when he had enough.

The gorilla had also woken up and decided to take a wander and find some breakfast. It didn't take him long to come across the hoard that the chimp was creating. The hungry gorilla began eating it, to the horror of the chimp.

"Oi! Get off of my fruit! Get your own!"

"Who's fruit?"

"My fruit, that's who's!"

"Come down here," shouted the gorilla, beckoning the chimp to descend from the canopy of trees.

"Get your own bloomin' fruit! That's mine!"

The chimp hurried down with quite a frown on his face, as he could see the gorilla munching on mangos, pears, berries and nuts. Once the chimp was on the floor, the gorilla stood up so he was broad and tall.

"Now then, you say this fruit is yours, but I see no name on them. So, I reasoned to myself, that they must be for everyone. If you can prove that you own them, I will apologize."

"Well, there's no name on them, but I gathered all of this, for me!"

The gorilla placed a hand on his chin, stroking it gently as he thought.

"Hmm, so you cannot prove it is yours. Well, it must be everyone's and anyone's then! Tell me, did I complain yesterday, when you ate the food I had gathered? No, I did not! Yet I kindly let you eat it, even though you never asked. Wouldn't it be more polite to ask rather than steal?"

The chimp thought about it, but had no answer.

"If you treat me in this way, I also have the right to treat you the same," said the gorilla. "So if you take from me, I'll take from you."

"But that's not right!"

"Why?"

"Well, I did all the hard work getting the food!"

"Yes, it was rather handy!"

"But it's mine!'

"Well learn this, young chimp; if you treat others this way, you should expect the same to happen to you! It's not nice is it, the way you are feeling? All this food that you worked hard for, taken by someone who never asked; it's not nice is it?"

"Er, well, no."

The gorilla moved forward and put his face right in front of the chimps, making himself rather intimidating. "No, it's not! Will you be doing this again?"

"No, I won't!"

"Good. Now go away so I can enjoy this fruit."

And the chimp moved along, having learnt his lesson, whilst the gorilla munched heartily on another mango.

The chimp carried himself off and walked rather forlornly along the trail, dragging his hands on the floor, with his bottom lip drooping so low that it might trip him over. All alone and enjoying his disappointed mood, the chimp grumbled to himself, wandering what could lift this feeling, when he happened upon a cheerful bird.

"Hullo, chum," said the bird, whilst twittering gleefully.

"Hi."

"Why you so glum, chum?"

"Oh, because..."

"Because...?"

"Just because."

The little, brightly coloured bird flew about then landed on a branch, nearer to the chimp.

"There's no need to be glum!"

"Yes, there is! I don't want to talk about it."

The bird turned its head quickly from side to side, blinking its bright eyes.

"Whenever I feel down, I turn my frown upside-down and I do so by singing this song; When I'm glum, I begin to hum, and the tune turns to a song. My mood lifts, rather swift, as I choose not to think on what it was that made me down... Then I sing,

"Biddle-ee-bop-shoo-de-wop,

riddle-dee-riddle-dee-dee,

Swing my wings, hear me sing,

Riddle-mee-riddle-mee-dee.

Hop-hop-skip-and-hop

Riddle-dee-riddle-dee-ree

Worry me not, not a jot,

Riddle-mee-riddle-mee-dee."

The little bird, skipped and hopped about singing its song merrily, then stopped and turned to watch the chimp, who sat doing nothing with a dull look on his face.

"Come on, stand up! Sing along!"

"No, I don't want to, it's stupid!"

"Well, you decide how you want to feel! It's up to you. You can choose to be down with a frown, or choose to turn it upside-down. Your choice!"

The chimp said nothing, continuing to look downwards and sulk, so the bird hopped over and started singing and dancing again, all the while encouraging the chimp to join in.

"I won't stop until you join in," sang the bird and then a very reluctant chimp got up and joined the dancing bird, singing with it,

"Biddle-ee-bop-shoo-de-wop,

riddle-dee-riddle-dee-dee,

Swing my wings, hear me sing,

Riddle-mee-riddle-mee-dee.

Hop-hop-skip-and-hop

Riddle-dee-riddle-dee-ree

Worry me not, not a jot,

Riddle-mee-riddle-mee-dee."

After a short while, the two were singing along quite happily and the chimp even started dancing! So much so that the chimp even started to enjoy himself, seeming to not have a care in the world.

A young boy was walking nearby and heard the noise of the chimp and bird. Being curious of the cacophony, he went over to see just what was going on and when he saw the singing bird and dancing chimp, he started laughing. The two animals were oblivious to the fact they were being observed for quite a while, that was until the chimp fell backwards accidentally, landing on his bottom.

"And who might you be?" asked the bird.

"I might be someone, but probably no one."

"That's a clever answer! I like that. So then, 'someone, but probably no one,' what are you doing spying on us?"

"I heard the noise and wondered what was happening, that's all."

"Have you got any food?" said the chimp, sidestepping around the boy, inspecting him from head to toe.

"I do not, I'm afraid."

"Why are you afraid?"

"Oh, I'm not really afraid, it's just an expression people use. I have nothing with me, but I am heading home and should have something to eat there. Did you want to come

The chimp gave a broad smile.

"I take it, that's a 'yes," laughed the child. "Come on then, follow me."

The chimp followed the boy and the bird followed the chimp, and together they walked to the child's home. As they left the forested jungle, they came to a clearing. In the distance, on the horizon, the dark brown tops of dry grass roofs could be seen, seeming so far away, yet so close at the same time. Walking through the ankle high grass they continued.

"This is taking a long time," exclaimed the chimp.

"We'll be there soon," replied the child. "We'll be there before night falls."

"Before night falls? Is the night really going to fall on us?"

"Well of course it is!"

"I better go and warn everyone! We can't have the night falling on everybody! It'll crush them all, and the trees, and bushes; think of the fruit it will crush! Then there will be just piles of fruity mush..."

"No, no, wait! It's just an expression..."

But it was too late, the chimp had started running away making a raucous noise, like a scream.

WHEN THE NIGHT FELL.

The chimp ran in to the jungle screaming and screeching.

"Ah! No! The night's going to fall on us," he shouted. "Everybody run! Hide!"

As the chimp whizzed about, all sorts of animals popped their heads up to see what all the noise was about.

"Everyone run! The night's falling on us! Hide!"

A tarantula crawled quickly from its hole to the top of a log. "What do you mean the night is falling?"

"That big thing, that's dark, it's falling on us!"

"Falling?"

"Yes! It'll crush us all, and everything; think of the fruit it will crush! Then there will be just piles of fruity mush..."

"My, my! That's not good! We better tell everyone!"

"I am! I am!"

The tarantula scuttled off to tell everyone and the chimp went back to screeching and shouting.

A panther, wondering what on earth was going on, approached the chimp. "Whatever is this hullabaloo? What's wrong with you?"

"That big thing, that's dark, it's falling on us! It'll crush us all, and everything; think of the things it will crush! Then we'll be just piles of mush..."

"Oh, you silly chimp! It's just an expression!"

"What? What do you mean?"

The panther shook her head from side to side, in disbelief. "The night isn't literally going to fall! It means that the sun is going to bed and the moon will be out instead. Nothing is going to fall down and 'crush us all to mush!' You silly monkey!"

"No?"

"No. Sometimes people say things in an expressive way, using similes or metaphors, instead of saying something literally. For example, as daft as a brush, means someone is a bit silly, but the person isn't a brush, are they? Or maybe you've heard someone say, 'as quiet as a mouse.' They may have been quiet, but not a mouse!"

"Oh! Well I never! That is mighty strange," said the chimp.

"How we use words can be confusing, but if you truly speak from the heart, people will understand."

"But my heart doesn't speak..."

"Speaking from the heart is when what you feel inside you is sent to the one you are speaking to. If you say things with a smile, people will see and hear that smile. And if you are sad, they will sense that also. It's not just what you say, but how you say it. Speak from the heart and those who listen will feel what you feel.

"Words have a power that is felt deeply. So choose your words wisely."

The chimp smiled as he listened to the panther, feeling comforted by what she was saying. Once the panther had finished, she placed a large paw on his shoulder to reassure him, then he jumped about happily.

As the daylight began to hide over the horizon, the noises of the jungle quietened, being replaced by the sounds of the night creatures. The chimp settled down in a cosy spot and started to shut his eyes. As he did so, a little spider crawled quickly about, up in the nearby tree. Gently it whizzed about, attaching it's silk from one spot to another. It was almost hypnotic, as the circular motion of the spider spun it's web from limb to leaf, leaf to tree, tree to branch and branch to limb. Then it fell, suddenly, and the chimp became worried as to where the spider had gone, however, the spider ascended back up, climbing a silky thread to where it fell from.

THE SPIDER'S WEB. *(For Margaret)*

"Are you alright?" asked the chimp.

"Oh, yes. I'm fine," replied the spider. "It takes practice to learn how to spin a web and I'm still learning."

"How do you learn?"

"Well, I take my thread and pass it from this point to another and if it sticks, I think, 'That's great!' And if it doesn't, I think, 'Oo, I better learn from my mistake.' Then I try somewhere else, starting again."

The spider resumed its crawl, moving swiftly from leaf to leaf, branch to stem, stem to leaf, leaf to leaf. And it carried on doing so, mesmerizing the chimp who was nearly asleep. It slipped again, then climbed back up, to continue going from leaf to leaf, branch to stem, stem to leaf, leaf to leaf, branch to stem, stem to leaf, leaf to leaf, branch to stem, stem to leaf, leaf to leaf until complete. After finishing, it moved to the upper right part of the web and wiped its head with its two from legs.

"Now I wait."

"Wait for what?" quizzed the entranced chimp.

"For a juicy moth or fly to get stuck in my web."

"How long do you wait?"

"As long as necessary. There is no time set for when it happens, it just happens when it happens."

"But aren't you hungry? I doubt I could wait for a long time for my food."

"Ah, but there is no time."

"No time? Of course there is! It took you all that time to weave your web, so surely there is time!"

"Oh no, my friend. For all the while I was spinning around, it appeared that time was passing by, even to you through your eyes. Yet I was focused only on the moment I was weaving my web and for me that moment is still happening now."

"You stopped making your web though," stated the confused chimp.

"Yes and that moment has passed, but all that time was just in your mind, for that moment is still now. As you recall that moment from the past, it is happening now, once again for you, so all is happening now."

The monkey gave a befuddled look and scratched his head.

"You only ever exist in this moment," continued the spider. "Where you are present, is the presence of the moment. A memory can be plucked from your mind, to be seen now. So did it occur in the past, or is it happening now? For it is present with you in this moment. Just think of it like this:

"Along an astral path,

Heading towards the unknown,

Leaving memories, like breadcrumbs,

So we many trace our way home.

Winding round the clockwork,

Our planet a gear in the works,

Our galaxy yet another cog

Of where time may lurk.

Movement within the stars,

Never static, moving forever in space,

Treading only once on a location,

Memory leaves a souvenir to trace.

Forever moving forward,

Creation bangs the gong,

Time no more a feature

For its illusion now is gone.

Living for each moment,

Existence ventures on,

Never stepping in the same river twice,

One wonders where it has gone.

It moves, it weaves, it always leaves

A memory to impart

of space-time now and forever,

Like a phantom in the dark.

What matter has been known,

Recycled endlessly, knowing what to do,

The atom, like a snowball,

Gathers memories on its way through

The universe and its moments,

Forever to impart,

Knowing just what to be

And exploring every path.

On our route through the universe,

One never stands on the same place twice,

For space-time marches on,

So pay heed to this advice;

From within the mind's eye,

You can perceive a memory,

Its location in time and space,

Are behind, laying in eternity.

Seek it and you will find

the secret of how space-time weaves

A memory within each atom,

How it transforms from flower into a leaf.

The cosmos fires memories,

Like stars through the night,

Along its synaptic pathways,

It learns and makes this existence bright.

This universal mind

Imparts the learning, like a mime,

Arriving like a spec of light,

As wave or particle, knowing ahead of time

What form it takes is necessary

To get to where it's going,

Along the road of memories,

It is powerful and all knowing."

Then the chimp closed its eye, falling asleep under the starry sky, as the tiny spider looked up at the bright moon, through the leafy canopy of the jungle. A moth flew into his web, getting caught in the stickiness.

"Things happen at just the right time," it said and scurried across to eat its supper.

Bioluminescent bugs and flying things, glowed in the jungle looking like shooting stars they moved. It was like a different world at night, with a different set of noises from the nocturnal creatures that awoke to the setting sun. Clouds that passed by, formed landscapes in the sky and its shadow moved like a hand, stroking nature gently, just as a mother would to soothe her child to sleep. And the conscious day made way to grant lease to the dreams of night.

As the moon made its way across the sky, gently guiding the sea, the breeze followed the way of the movement and turned to breathe over the jungle's trees.

A tiny frog was sitting by a small pool of water, contemplating where the day had disappeared to. It was just sitting there letting thoughts come and go, as they do, but she was wondering what had happened to the sun; where had it gone? So she turned to the bat that was hanging about and said,

"What happened to the daytime? Where has the sun gone? Where does it hide at night?"

"It has not gone anywhere, its spirit is still here," replied the bat.

"Whatever do you mean?

SPIRIT. *(For Peter)*

The bat flew from where it had been perched upside down and landed on a log, somewhere near the ground.

"How can the sun's spirit be here? The sun has hidden itself away," said the curious, tiny frog.

"The sun has not hidden itself, it's merely spun to the other side of the world. Where it is now, it is day to them which means it is night to us. Yet its spirit is still present."

"How?"

"The moon you see has no light of its own, for it reflects the sun's light, so at night we can still see. The moon is not the sun, but it's the spirit of the sun that encourages it to reflect the light."

The tiny frog thought about this but was now even more curious.

"What is spirit made of?" asked the frog.

"What's it made of? Well, it's like the wind; the moon guides the tide, and the waters of the tide guide the wind. Yet what is the wind made from? Where does it come from? Where does it go? It simply is the wind. We know its presence by feeling it blow, we feel its motion, we know it's there, yet we can only see it as it brushes the trees, the hairs on people's heads, grass in the field rippling like waves, heads of flowers bowing and nodding to its movement. So we observe the wind by noticing its effect on other things.

"It does not speak, but we hear it blow. It is not visible, but we see its show upon the fields, trees and grass; we know its presence by its effect. It is like the very breath you breathe in and out, for you know it's there without a doubt, but can you grasp and catch it? Can you say from where it came? Can you tell me where it goes? It simply is breath.

"This is spirit and all have it. Not only do you and I have spirit, but so does creation, the universe and it is the spirit that binds everything together."

"So I have a spirit?"

"Oh yes, my dear. And then there's the great spirit, the force, which some call the universe. Others give it many names, but it is the first that came about, that gave

existence to life itself. This great power of creation keeps creating, whether flowers, rain, frogs or bats. It gives birth and let's things be what they will be."

This got the frog thinking even harder and so many questions formed in her mind. Plucking one from thought she asked, "Did it also create good and bad?"

The bat flew about to stretch its wings then landed back down next to the frog.

"Now, my dear, that's an interesting question! The choices made, either good or bad, are within us. The spirit made everything and gave us the power of choice, so good and bad things come from us.

"There will always be a natural order of things, for this is the spirit's way of ensuring order within the chaos of our choices."

"A natural order?"

"Well, yes! Everything is born, everything can create, everything dies. Seasons change, plants grow, reproduce and die. No matter how much you try to bend the order, you cannot, for all things live and die. Yet the spirits of all exist, like stars in the sky.

"Many of the stars you see, are burnt out suns that once looked like ours! However, they have died and their light lingers on. So all things have spirit, all things are born, live, reproduce and die, only to live on as spirit in the memory of the universe.

"So, my dear, when the idea of bad things is made from choice, the natural order ensures that this will pass by and die. For ultimately, the force, the spirit, is good, giving lease to opportunity and choice, but makes sure that its way, the natural order of things, conquers darkness with light. For light always gets to where it wants to be, either by shining bright, or reflecting on a moon in the night. It always gets from here to there, whether it's in physical appearance or by spirit, as it knows and sees all, for it cares."

As the bat finished talking, it looked up to the sky and the tiny frog turned her head also to see the grandeur of the night sky's flickering starlight, shooting stars crying out, "I am here," as they departed to dust. Then a gentle gust of wind brushed their brows and they bowed their heads to acknowledge the presence of something greater, that they could not see, but sense.

As morning dawned, the scenery changed, as if the curtain in a theatre had been lifted, revealing the new stage of daylight. Birds sang of the good morning and the nocturnal creatures retired to sleep.

"Good morning! Good morning," shouted a loud voice.

The macaque turned to look at where the noise was coming from.

"Oh, not you again! You're always getting on my nerves!"

An anteater was smiling and singing to the sky, "Good morning! Good morning! Thank you sun for dawning! Good morning, good morning to you! Good morning, good morning, thank you sun for dawning, good morning, good morning, to you and you and you and you!!"

"You're always happy, aren't you!?"

"It's a wonderful day," replied the anteater.

GRATITUDE.   *(For Samiska)*

"Good morning! Good morning! Thank you sun for dawning! Good morning, good morning to you! Good morning, good morning, thank you sun for dawning, good morning, good morning, to you and you and you and you," sung the anteater as he continued to greet his friends who were waking up.

The macaque shook his head, thinking about the joy that was being spread by the irritating, yet happy, anteater who was still being a missionary for the morning sun.

"Will you shut up!"

"No, I won't, for it's another beautiful day. The sky is bright, everyone is happy and well, it's just an elegant morning."

"What if it was raining?"

"Then I'd be glad of the rain, bringing its refreshing dance, creating a rainbow in the sky and let's not forget, it's great to get wet!"

"Oh good grief! You're always happy. There must be something that doesn't make you happy."

"No, not a thing!"

"Getting stung by a plant, that must make you unhappy..."

"Makes me feel alive."

"How about getting bitten by an insect?"

"Well, it may not make me happy, but it certainly doesn't make me sad!"

"Someone steals your food...."

"Then they won't go hungry!"

"An elephant treads on your foot..."

"Oh it might hurt, but doesn't mean that I'm not happy!"

Not a thing could cancel the joy of the anteater, he was just so full and abundant with happiness, effervescent by simply spreading the good news of goodness.

"How can you possibly be happy all the time?" asked the macaque.

"Happiness is a choice. When things happen, it's your choice to be glum or be happy. When you frown, you are down, so turn the frown upside down. Have a smile, laugh a while and always remember, gratitude is an attitude and it's the best one to have..."

"You're not going to sing again are you? Close your ears, everyone!" advised the macaque.

Then the anteater began singing his song;

"Gratitude is the best attitude

For it's always best to be happy.

Without an attitude of gratitude,

You tend to seem rather shabby.

Gratitude is the best attitude

And it's very good for the mind

For an attitude without gratitude,

Tends to be miserably inclined.

Gratitude is the best attitude,

It's a test of feeling glad.

Without gratitude as your attitude,

You'd be glum, low or mad.

An attitude of gratitude

Should be displayed when someone's giving,

Saying, "Thanks!" with a big smile

Is good for every being.

The attitude of gratitude

Brings thanks into your voice.

And gratitude being your attitude,

Is really a matter of choice.

And remember, within any experience,

Whether it's been good or bad,

With an attitude such as gratitude,

It was one you may otherwise never have had.

Developing a gratitude attitude,

Enriches your very self.

And with a positive attitude

Comes the very best of health.

It's the biggest decision you make,

To have a positive disposition,

For the attitude of gratitude

Saves many from derision.

So when you're feeling down,

Or when you're feeling sad,

Remember gratitude is the best attitude

One can ever really have."

All the animals clapped their hands, stamped their feet, whistled or called out, "encore!" as the anteater took a bow.

"More! More!"

"Encore!"

The anteater closed his eyes, then opened them and started singing once more.

"With an attitude of gratitude

You can never really be glum,

For with the gratitude attitude,

One always tends to hum

This little tune to take you through the day

'Cos with gratitude as your attitude

You chase negativity away.

To keep the optimistic attitude

Listen to that little voice,

That asks, 'Are you happy, or are you sad?'

For this is always your choice.

So choose to be happy,

Every single day,

And with gratitude as your attitude,

You'll chase the blues away!"

Once again, applause and shouts of appreciation roused the jungle and even the macaque had a smile on his face.

"You silly thing! That was absolutely stupid and daft, but I liked it," said the smiling macaque.

The Abbot concluded his tale, so the monks stood up and began to leave the hall, all muttering and talking about the lessons to be gleaned from his tale.

"How is he so wise?" asked one monk to another.

"Some say he found wisdom in a book that's hidden far away," replied another.

The conversation played on a certain monk's mind. This certain monk was called, Sasha and he went about his business, keeping his mind occupied with thoughts of the Abbot's wisdom and rumours of the book. Days passed and his mind kept wondering if it could be true, that there might be one book that contained all the wisdom of the world.

As Sasha continued his daily chores, he was mindful of the wonderful stories that the Abbot had told. Going to his cell, he decided that it was now his mission to obtain the knowledge and wisdom of his elders. Stealing himself away from sleep that night, he went in search of the elders. They were sitting together in a chapel, talking about things that elders do.

The Book of Books. *(For Idries)*

"Excuse me please," began Sasha. "I have decided that I must seek, not only the knowledge of the elders, but their wisdom. Please, put me on the right path and guide me to the source."

"Stay here and continue to learn," said Father Martin.

"I should do, but someone has said at all the wisdom of the world is contained in a book, somehow, somewhere."

"A book? I doubt if a single book could contain all the wisdom of the world," said Father Peter.

"But it has been said that there is such a book."

The elders looked at each other with curiosity. A few muted mutterings were made until Father Bear looked at the young monk, saying, "I think you're talking of the Book of Books, aren't you?"

"I don't know its name, just of this book of wisdom. I have heard much talk of its knowledge and how whoever reads it becomes wiser. Even the Abbot had read it, so I'm told."

The Abbot creased his face and said, "I have never ventured for this book, nor read its contents! Whoever told you that has gotten it very wrong indeed!"

Father Bear stood up and nodded to the other elders present.

"My boy, we have seen over the last two years your progression and how well you are doing, as well as how you are, er... 'becoming.' Why now do you seek something that ports to hold all the world's wisdom?"

Sasha lowered his head and replied, "Father, I am not saying that a person, such as I, can contain all the wisdom, but if a book can, then I am intrigued by its very presence, its history and contents. Let me seek it out, so we can share it with everyone."

"I expect it doesn't even exist! It's merely a myth," said Father Martin.

Father Bear however, squinted slightly and said, "I wouldn't be so sure of that, for I have heard of this myth and the most likely location of where it is. I have never had such fancy for seeking it out, but if it is true, then I agree with Brother Sasha, that we should find it and share it with all."

"If it's hidden away, maybe it's for good reason," said Father Martin.

Peter, the other elder who had spoken few words, agreed with Bear saying, "I agree with Father Bear. And we can also put to rest any myths, if it turns out not to be true, can't we?"

So it was agreed, that Sasha would go and search for the secret book. Not much was known as to where the book was located, save rumours and rumours of rumours, which collectively seemed enigmatic. One person mentioned it was in a hidden box, another said it was in a hidden temple, and yet another said it was in a cave under a cliff at the edge of the desert. So what little information they had was given to Sasha.

Father Bear told him, "Look for the mountains past the desert and head for them. At the bottom of these mountains are caves. There is a hidden cave and in this cave you will find a hidden temple and within the temple is a hidden vault. In the vault is a hidden box and in the box is the book."

Early next morning, as the sun was dawning, Sasha made his way out of the monastery, before his brethren awoke. Carrying only a rolled up blanket and begging bowl, he made his way, travelling first through the forest. As he moved through the forest and its trees, he found the path that had been formed naturally for it had been walked by many.

Following it along, he came across a stone bridge and decided to rest a while. After finding some berries and edible leaves, he ate to replenish his strength, whilst he sat beside the bridge. Animals travelled over, as did the odd pedestrian, making their way from there to here and some going from here to over there. Sasha could hear the feet and was quickly able to discern between bare foot, four feet, sandalled feet, hooves and leather shoes. Many other sounds were about alerting him to the variety of creatures about. Soon the noises became unidentifiable, as they merely became 'just sounds' and the mesmerizing nature about him became a subtle daze. In all his training and all his days at the monastery, he had never felt so at peace until now. The gentle breeze, buzzing flies, flapping wings, barks and cries, tweets and chirrups, panting and breathing, chattering and calling, all became as one; it was the sound of creation and it was almost if the creator was speaking through it all in a subtle whisper that could be heard but not understood. It reminded him of when visitors came to the monastery and even though they may not share the same tongue, they understood each other. In this unspoken understanding, Sasha sat listening to the message.

The sun had moved significantly lower in the sky and it suddenly became apparent to him, so he stood up, dusted himself down and went over the stone bridge. As he did so he began to see the distant tips of the mountains that seemed inexplicably close, yet were still a way off, as if some optical illusion had beset him. Knowing that he needed to head east, he continued onward, not detouring north as many did. First he needed to pass through the jungle and reach the furthest mountains, not meet the nearest, smaller ones that lay nearby with the foothills. There were caves there, one in which a magician was alleged to live, but these were not the caves he had in mind, nor the ones advised by the monastic elders. No, these caves were older and it had been said many times that under these ancient caves lay many tunnels, etchings and drawings, being a veritable labyrinth where people once lived and hid in colder, icy times, when the sun was unfriendly to the lands and dense, dark clouds courted rain and snow instead. Many myths surrounded the caves, including those of the Book of Books.

After finding a decent spot to rest, he bent some long branches down to secure a shelter and placed huge leaves over them. He placed his begging bowl just outside though, so moisture and rain could gather. In another large leaf, pollen was gathered from neighbouring trees, as well as some ready to eat legumes. Climbing the trees, one could find many things to eat, if you knew what to look for. Sasha had such knowledge and made good use of it, for in a short time he had gathered a large leaf plate of food and made several small leaf parcels, each containing naturally delicious foods. Once supper had been eaten, he unwrapped his blanket and decided to bed down for the night.

It took one and a half days to get through the forest and meet the jungle. To navigate the jungle would take at least another four days, yet Sasha knew where to head and had his course in mind.

"Look for the mountains past the desert and head for them. At the bottom of one of these mountains are caves. There is a hidden cave and in this cave you will find a hidden temple and within the temple is a hidden vault. In the vault is a hidden box and in the box is the book," Father Bear had said, his words echoing through dozy dreams as sleep approached.

He would not have to traverse the desert much at all, merely touch on it for maybe a day, just to get to the mountains and cliffs. If one could hear water, then they knew that they were too close to the jungle, thus it was the lack of hearing flowing water which meant you were approaching the mountain range via the desert. Once at the cliffs, the welcoming sound of gently flowing water would indicate you were on the right trajectory.

And in his mind, the journey was being planned, bringing back many childhood memories of being with his dad whilst hunting, traveling and discovering. He recalled memories with the traders also, as they made their way from place to place selling cloth, herbs, spices, rare foods, scents, perfumes, exquisite gems and remedies. The one overriding memory that came was the gossip of the caravan; who was doing what, where so'n'so was, who had turned up here & there, and what the latest news was, which more often than not about various philosophies, spiritual thought and beliefs. On these journeys, people often gathered together at night, to share fire, or find protection in greater numbers, and as they ate, drank and talked about different cultures, they shared stories and passed on advice. Collectively, these people were not just traders, but also missionaries from various beliefs, adventurers, courtiers travelling between kingdoms & queendoms, or those who were just curious about what was over that river, over that mountain, beyond the horizon and these meeting points were of great value which transcended monetary value. Some of these inns were built on these locations and along major routes. Yet here he was now, letting his mind idle as he wound down to sleep

Next day, he left the small shelter he'd made and went further into the jungle. Remembering the paths taken in his youth, he found some to be still in use, but others where less trodden and were harder to make out. Familiar noises became recognisable and smells triggered memories; scents of certain flowers reminded him of particular hunts for food, the petrichor aura of damp bacteria and moisture, brushed leaves which brought freshness; then there was the smell of death with its surrounding flies, sweet smells intoxicating insects to be a meal, pheromones attracting mates, and pungent odours where animals had left their markers making the wanderer aware. All of these things had been taught to him and as he navigated the jungle, if came flooding back to him. Deciding not to bed down in the jungle that night, he continued in the dark, cracking branches loudly which in turn made creatures of the night flee and make an array of sounds. Although it was night, the land did not become fully dark, for the evening left a lingering light until late and within the three hours of lucid light, the sun began to replace the subtle glow of the misty moon, as it began to rise into the starry sky, replacing the usurper of the fake dawn, a planet which shone brightly at first daylight. Gradually the daystar swung high into the heavens and the shift changed for the animals, for many sauntered to rest as others began to stir. Onward he went with gratitude towards the eternal light and headed for the edge of the desert, which was a weird and curious piece of land that was neither meadow, forest nor savannah. It was where the heat shouted loudly at the land and in response, the lush greenery progressively withdrew as the sun ruled with authority.

The air lost its humidity and patches of yellow, straw-like grass became more frequent. Leaving the last of the jungle, he broke large stems from plants and carried them like rods of wood on his shoulder, leaves pointing downwards, for he knew a trick or two to help aid travel, brief as it was, over the desert. As sand began to rapidly replace soil, he saw the sun moving to the southwest and decided to veer slightly north, for he had avoided the northern shortcut to go over the mountains, yet needed to be at a certain point where they began. The other trail, which avoided the jungle, followed the smooth rise through the hills and minor mountains, and was easy to achieve, as well as being the most popular route for traveling the mountain range. For Sasha, knowing that most of the caves were in fact within the cliffs on the adjacent side was a good hint at where any mystery cave may be.

"There is a hidden cave and in this cave you will find a hidden temple and within the temple is a hidden vault. In the vault is a hidden box and in the box is the book."

The words reverberated in his mind, as well as a memory of stories about certain ascetics who went to the mountains and lived in caves. He recalled one in particular regarding how one monk had been initiated into a particular lineage by the practice of building a wall in front of the cave entrance, so they could practice 'colour meditation' within. The absence of light created illusions in the mind, leading to other insights, deeper knowledge of the inner secrets of the order the monk was affiliated to and according to myth, even helped with the restoration of the physical body upon death. Some, in fact very few, had witnessed a few monks looking younger as they prepared to depart this realm, after they had performed this meditative isolation within the dark. As a monk himself, Sasha understood the irony of finding the light within darkness, as alluded to in these tales, but didn't believe the myths about how after these dark meditations, one was considered to have the power over weather, have sorcerous ways, magical powers and abilities beyond human ability. No, for him there was no magic, but entrancing tales to entertain children at night and travellers around a camp fire. Sasha believed in the supernatural, but not magic per se. Yet, he headed towards the mountains, the cliff side, the rough side, where once flat ground had been rent upwards, torn and thrust from the crust to form the range of mountains. On this side, clear evidence showed in natural display the levels of history cast within strata of differing colours, layers upon layers of the past sandwiched remains, fossils, bones, trees, dirt and tales of times rich in heritage that were unspoken, before man trod the earth and as he approached, these shades of yellow, red and brown began to slowly, but steadily, arise in the distance from the desert floor.

Becoming thirsty, he took one of the long stems from his shoulder and broke it sharply on his knee and twisted it slightly so the juices within flowed into his mouth, refreshing his palate. He had nothing with him to eat, but the fluid from the long cane was sweet and full of energy, certainly enough to carry him until evening. And when the day began to even out, the sun bowed its head passing a salutation to the night, thus the moon took its place in the east of the skyline.

Finding a suitable place on the desert floor, he made rest a priority, near a small rock formation that had sand on its top, leaning with other rocks towards the south, indicating the prevailing winds must come from the north. This small shelter would be enough should any wind whip itself up in the night and blow a chill air upon him. Wrapping himself in the blanket and laying on his side, he noticed the sheer magnificence and magnitude of the stars in the dark blue hue above him. Daylight was trying to keep an eye over the night in the far corner of his eye, but as he looked up he realised how many stars he could see; thousands, if not millions of them. What makes the night dark? Sasha thought about it and wondered if it was the absence of light, but realised this couldn't be so, for light was above him in the stars. He had a revelation about how the bodies in the heavens created the dark from their shadows, but actually the cosmos was extraordinarily light, each star lighting a way and where it met a physical body, shadow caused the dark universe. Likewise, the shadow of the moon caused the night upon the earth, but the reflection of light from the moon's surface broke the chains of shadow. As the moon rays met his eyes, he had another thought: although the sun was not seen at the moment, it was always present, whether as itself in daytime, reflected by moon at night, or even as light on his body, face and in his eyes. Should he close his eyes, then the absence of light may be apparent, yet it did not mean it was not there, just due to him not seeing it, for it was always there. Wasn't it? These thoughts accompanied Sasha to his slumber and soon his contemplation became invaded with other thoughts that became floating ideas in his mind, guiding them from dreams to the unconscious rest of the body. His mind however, was fully awake and it began arranging the library of thoughts, perceptions and ideas in dreams, containing images, possibilities, sounds and scenes as yet experienced in physical form.

In his dream, he saw a tree and the tree had been felled. It was stripped bare of bark, then turned into paper, bound in a book and sealed. No hand touched it, but it manifested and descended into a box, which closed its lid, and span down a long chamber until a grand wooden door closed it within, at the entrance where his mind's eye spied it. Looking for the gatekeeper, he saw only himself and he smiled at himself, as if he was somehow detached from his self for a fraction of a moment, looking at his own self as another person would. It was no reflection, it was Sasha seeing himself, for just a flicker of a second. Stirring slightly from sleep, he opened his eyes to receive more of the sun's light proffered by the moon, then closed them again. The image of another person came to mind immediately, but he knew not who it was and unable to discern between dream or vision, he chose the dream and his tired body took him to the land of sleep.

The next day, he continued on as a harsh wind from the north blew the sand, whipping it around like a sling to fire thousands of miniscule stones in the direction of his skin. Sasha tried to cover his eyes from the onslaught, but whatever he did he was unsuccessful, for such was the strength in the wind. Walking ever onward towards the cliff side of the mountains, he was looking forward to the refuge they offered from samoon that whistled about him, for it was draining his energy to walk against the wind. It was like walking up a hill with a force pushing against you, tiring the arms as you attempt to push back and causing leg muscles to ache due to the extra energy needed to move against the invisible foe. Sasha's sight was impaired so much that he could not see the distance easily and needed to find somewhere to stop, establish the landscape and make sure he was on course. Time passed and eventually he went past the open land where the wind was strongest, meaning he was closer to the cliff face. Being able to see more clearly, he searched the landscape, established the mountains and headed directly towards them. The distant shapes loomed and started to show their rugged formation, the magnificence of their presence and harsh character. Like giant asymmetric, mute beasts, they grew in size with every step he took. Soon, he began to hear the faintest trickle of water and knew he was on track.

Gradually Sasha saw the caves ahead and they looked like bizarre stone animals with their mouths wide open, waiting to be fed. Some of them were small, but the majority were vast catacombs, a maze of adventure. Where one continent slammed into the other, the stone and earth had been pushed up to form the mountains and the desert side of them had been the force that had pushed the other plate upwards, forming the rugged face of the range. At the base of the mountains, where the collision occurred, the caves had been initially formed then time's weathering had sculpted the entrances. The insides had been worked and carved by mankind as curiosity drove them further inwards. The network of caves was substantially vast, housing many secrets. Just how far into the earth they went, no one truly knew. Once they provided shelter, thus many people had used them regularly, but these days no one seemed to reside there, or at least that was what most thought.

"There is a hidden cave and in this cave you will find a hidden temple..." These words came to mind as Sasha drew closer.

A sense of accomplishment began to arise, but it was a false sense, for the true object of his quest was not with him yet. And where should he start? What cave should he enter first?

Meeting the huge cliff face of the mountains, Sasha stopped for breath, contemplation and rest. He could see at least seven major entrances and pondered on which one to investigate first. Deciding to follow a logical process, he decided on working his way from left to right, so walked westward until he could enter the first mammoth opening. The sun lit up the entrance well and aided his inspection as he sauntered along viewing chiselled walls and eroded rock. The cavern narrowed the further he went in, until he came to an abrupt end, where dark earth hinted at historic fires that had kept visitors warm. So in to the second cave he went, again tracing the walls which were more rugged and revealed many layers of history. The sandy brown colours were interlaced with dark grey and pale, whiter layers nearer the top of the walls. This cave was particularly deep and went on for a while, until it branched into two. Going down the left path, he came to a dead end quickly, so returned to the fork and took the other passage, but again he had no success in finding anything. The same was with the third and fourth caves, but the fifth bore some interest.

As he went in the fifth cave mouth, there were feint marks on the walls that looked like line drawings. Further along, he saw some tributaries and examined each of them. One in particular had handprints on the walls and remnants of fire ash on the ground. The shadows of the past reached out to tell him that people had been here seeking shelter. Small and large hands revealed possibly a father and son once sought refuge here, like Sasha and his dad had done when he was younger, as he learnt the way of the hunter and how to survive in the different environments.

Moving down another passage, he found a burnt out torch on the wall, next to a faded, yet colourful drawing of a man's profile holding something in his hands. It was hard to make sense of the picture, but it drew Sasha further along, where he came across flickering shadows that hinted of something, possible someone, within the cave. The shadows became larger as he got closer and eventually he discovered a torch that was still alight. Looking around, he saw more drawings of men and women all drawn in profile, all looking and walking in the same direction. The walls were all painted red as well, showing strong evidence of occupation within the cavern. Following the direction of the faces, he moved further within the mountain until he came across a large wooden door with iron hinges and handle. Curiosity drove him to open up the creaky, old door.

Inside it looked like a chapel, with an altar carved into the rock wall on one side and a large faded picture of a woman sitting down in front of a tree, which made up most of the scene, on the wall immediately in front of him. Traces of gold leaf could be seen on the sun behind the tree and muted bronze, brown and green explained the objects of the depiction. It portrayed a scene familiar to Sasha, of a story he'd heard a few times when was a child about how a woman had stolen the sun and kept it in a tree, basically explaining how plants need light and the cycle of nature. The picture though had a heavily faded area in the middle, as if hands had smudged it over a period of time. Enticed by it, Sasha went over to feel the picture, like so many others had done before him. When his hands touched, it felt as if one could push it and so he did.

The wall was actually a large painted door which opened to reveal a large chamber, bathed in light. Gold walls reflected firelight and within the chamber were four people, three girls and a man. One of the girls was dressed in fine robes of scarlet and turquoise and she smiled as she noticed the visitor. Sasha wasn't sure that this was all real and shook his head.

"It's alright, come in, come in," said the girl.

"What is this place?" Sasha looked about and saw more people lurking a little further back.

"Welcome to the temple of light. I am glad you found us, for not many do."

Looking around, he saw people reclined on couches, eating food and drinking. The walls had many murals relating scenes of untold tales.

"I'm looking for a temple within these caves that houses a book, a book of wisdom."

"This is not that temple," said the priestess. "This is the temple of light. Whomsoever comes here gains eternal life. Come and join us...."

Sasha was amazed and walked further into the temple. The amount of light in the room was almost blinding and his eyes needed to adjust after being in the dim, torch-lit cavern.

"Eternal life? How?"

"We hold the secrets of eternity here."

"Is this it? Is this the place where the Book of Books resides?"

"No, my friend that is in another temple, but come, sit and refresh yourself."

Thoughts raced through his head and he was tempted to stay here. The bountiful tables and ornaments lured him further into the temple chamber. He now knew

he was close to the temple where the book was and knew it was real, but it was not in this place.

"I cannot stay. I am on a quest for the Book of Books, but tell me, how do I gain eternal life?"

"In order to be granted immortality, you must join us, learn from us and receive the transmission from the tree of life."

"So I must stay here to gain immortality. This I cannot do, for I must find the book. Where is it?"

"I do not know, but it is within these caves."

He felt so close to finding the book, but the attraction of staying here to learn the secrets of eternal life was attractive to him. Deciding his mind, Sasha turned to leave.

"I thank you for your offer, but I must find the Book of Books," he said and then left the temple.

As he left, the painted door closed behind him and he returned to the dimly lit caves. Exiting the chapel, he went straight to the cave entrance and decided to enter the sixth one. Once more, the stony walls led him within the mountain and after a short while, drawings similar to the other cavern appeared. These ones had mainly young men facing inside the cave, holding a staff in each of their hands. More drawings revealed the moon and shadows being cast on the men as they approached the moon. Long, dark shadows grew in length as he walked ever onwards until he came to another chapel, an open one, with an altar made from a sandy type of stone that had dusty metal plates upon it. Behind the altar was a mural of people holding staffs aloft, with the moon pouring out light, like water from a chalice, that was held by a figure that was giant like, with a tricorner hat upon his head. Moving towards it, Sasha looked for a door, thinking that the entrance was similar to the other temple, but he could not find one. That was until he noticed that all the shadows in the mural were pointing towards one point. Looking around, he saw a dark stone inserted on floor that seemed out of place. He placed a foot upon it and at once a door opened from the rock wall.

Inside the temple was bathed in silver light and revealed no person within, that was until he walked further in and a shadow appeared to approach him. The person then revealed their physical self, emerging from the shadow and bowed before Sasha.

"Welcome, welcome! It's nice to greet you. What is it you seek?"

"I'm searching for the Book of Books. Is it here?"

The tall man had a gentle face and long silvery, black hair. He looked over Sasha, as if inspecting him.

"No, this is not where the Book of Books is kept, that is within another temple under the mountain."

"Then what is this place?"

The silver light had a hint of blue within it, simulating the colour of moonlight. Sasha looked around to see more people revealing themselves from their shadowy forms and getting closer. All held a staff, except the host, but he wore a long cloak and cowl, it's hood not covering his head but resting on the shoulders. The dark blue and grey robes covered his body completely.

"This is the temple of shadows, where we keep the sacred texts of the Magus. We protect the magic of the sorcerer who transmits the knowledge to the chosen few. Have you come to join us and learn the sorcery of the Magus?"

"No. I merely seek the Book of Books. Do you know where it is kept? Can you guide me there?"

"I cannot, for I have not been there, but we can teach you the arts of sorcery so you can find it. We hold tremendous power, bestowed upon us by the Magus and you also can have this if you stay with us."

Once again, Sasha was tempted to learn these powers, the dark arts, as he called them, but.... A thought came to mind that maybe he could learn them and use them for good.

"Tell me about this power the Magus has."

"It is as old as the universe itself and has been harnessed only by a few. The Magus knows how to tame this force by sorcery, so it can be used to exact revenge, bring control over people's minds and wills. We know of the secret methods, but await the inner teachings from our master," began the tall host, explaining further of the power within this mysterious force.

Sasha began to notice similarities between the sorcery and things he had learnt from the traders he'd travelled with when he was younger; tricks used within language, so people could be coerced to buy goods; how to play with someone's mind so that they were hypnotized and entranced to do things they may not otherwise do. Then the shadow-like priest told of tricks played upon the eye, illusions and sleight of hand, which some would call entertainment, for they diverted attention from what was really was going on.

Then the priest began explaining about this mysterious spirit, that been around since the dawn of time. Sasha likened it to faith, the laws of reciprocity and attraction.

"There is an art of how to master control over this spiritual force, so it can be, be... manipulated to control things; weather, fire, water, earth, wood & rock, people and situations," concluded the priest and demonstrated his control over the fiery torches in the moonlit temple cave. Drawing dragons, zephyrs, salamanders and hitherto as yet unknown beasts from the flames, his skills impressed Sasha.

"But why would you want to control these things?"

He was indeed curious to know why anyone would want to possess such powers and the grey sorcerer answered, "There are times when people do not do as you want them to do, so to make sure they do what you want, we employ these techniques."

"It all seems like cheap tricks and illusion, which I've seen before. And this mysterious force you speak of, it sounds like mesmerism and more illusions. Surely you must know of faith and it's power, and that it cannot be tamed. It works with and through us. We cannot force it."

Suddenly, a large dark shadow came from one of the temple's aisles, growing larger with every step, then its booming voice said, "Who is this that believes not in the teachings of the Magus?"

Sasha was not impressed by the presence, for he knew the tricks needed to create such a menacing presence. Raising his hands in front of the torch he moved them until they too became large, then pulled the hood down off of the Magus's head. A decrepit, older man smiled at Sasha.

"Ah, so we have a new apprentice!"

"No, I have no desire to stay and learn tricks. There is no magic; there's only trickery, mind tricks and illusions. I agree that there is a spirit within the universe that we can call upon, but I think it would be a brave man who thinks he can harness and tame it!"

The Magus laughed.

"Well there's no fooling this young man! Is there? What is it you're seeking then?"

"I'm searching for the Book of Books. I believe it is in these caves."

"Indeed it is young sir! Which cave and where, I do not know, for I have never sought wisdom, but entertained kings, queens and those who can afford these, let us say darker arts, that we perform. Come and learn the inner teachings from us..."

Sasha looked at the Magus with curiosity, for he seemed to understand the skills he was using were simple tricks and illusions, yet Sasha was intrigued by the mysterious spirit, the power of the universe, and wondered if he may learn more about it from the magicians.

"You mention the spirit and that it's as old as time, and I would want to know more about this."

"There is a power, a force that one can learn that brings incredible evil or profound goodness," said the Magus. "If you believe in this ability, to either cause harm or good, then you will find it. The people who seek us do not spend the time contemplating the power, they want someone who has done this and can do it for them instead. Yet, anyone who silences the mind can see and hear the power at work in nature, life and themselves."

"I have spent most of my adult life learning to silence the mind and have heard of this spirit, we refer to it as something else, faith."

"Ah! The great faith in the supreme."

"Supreme what?"

"Well, that's up for debate! Yet however one perceives it, there does appear to be a mysterious power at work. Some believe, others do not, but all our magic is down to belief."

"Pardon me for saying so, but with all due respect, your magic is a mix of tricks, illusion and this belief."

The Magus laughed. "It is true! But this belief that we can do the seemingly impossible is due to the nature of the universe, of this I am sure. You would make an excellent apprentice, young man. Why don't you stay with us? Learn more about the secrets of 'magic."

Sasha looked to the exit, paused then turned back to the grand wizard.

"No, I thank you, but no. I am resolute in my quest and must find the book."

"The Book of Books,' said to contain all the wisdom of the world... I hope you find it. I have not sought wisdom, for it found me. I wish you well on your adventure."

And with that, the Magus led Sasha to the door and escorted him out into the chapel area. Bidding farewell to him, he made his way to the cliff face and entered the next set of caves.

The main passage was duller than the previous ones, due to the light travelling down across the sky, but it revealed enough for Sasha to find his way to the belly of the maze. Along one passage, he saw pictures of people portrayed as shadows, with animals near them that bore good resemblance to their living relations. They had fine features unlike the shadowy drawings of presumable hunters and hand prints outlined in ochre displayed a history of dwellers who had sought shelter within the labyrinth of caves. Soon the tell-tale signs of torchlight crept along the tunnel walls and he wondered who maintained them; who would take the time to replenish torches on the off chance of someone possibly walking down these hallowed halls? "Must be the priests and residents of the temples within," he thought. His thought was actually vocal and he could hear a subtle echo bounce away from him. Mixed in to the echo was a low trickle, indicating water was nearby. As he progressed towards the sound, it became louder and soon he found himself in front of a small underground river, that flowed further inward and under the mountains. Its waters came from a modest waterfall and were an azure colour due to the lack of sunlight and a hint of green emanated from within the flow. Cupping his hands, Sasha drank a little to make sure it was fine to drink and it was, as well as refreshing, chilled, able to quench his thirst. The sapphire liquid ran over his hands as he drank. Moving towards the waterfall, he noticed a narrow ledge enabling entrance into an almost hidden passage behind the falling waters. Placing his back against the wall, he moved sideways along the ledge carefully and entered the slim cave behind the waters that formed the waterfall. Lured inwards, Sasha walked a little then turned to stop and watch the cascading flow of the waterfall.

After some time, he came across a drawing of a man sitting at what appeared to be a bench or table, looking as if he was writing, or in thought, or both. The painting was more recent than the others, the colours having a fair hue, not vibrant, yet not faded. Moving a little further forward, he saw a small alcove and in it a timber door with brass fittings. Intrigued, he opened it and stepped into a small room which housed a table and chair. There was nothing else, just this simple furniture, not even a torch. Having looked about, Sasha left the room and moved on, coming to another room identical to the last. Moving further still, he found two more rooms the same, but at the end of the dark passage, he was met by a wooden door that was ajar. A flickering yellowish red, light licked the air inviting him in and in he went.

In the middle of the room was a table with a man sitting over it, writing in a book. He didn't stir, merely keeping his quill on the page as he continued writing.

"Is this where the Book of Books resides?"

The man did not reply, but pointed his idle hand towards a door in the corner. Again it was a simple, wooden door that opened to reveal a humble, modest temple of stone pillars, little light and a high altar. The feint sound of a monotonous tone came from somewhere that wasn't human, but like something was vibrating, resonating. Observing the temple aisles, Sasha walked around remembering the words of Father

Bear, "There is a hidden cave and in this cave you will find a hidden temple and within the temple is a hidden vault. In the vault is a hidden box and in the box is the book."

After searching, he came across a door leading to a corridor with 3 more doors on each side. Turning the first handle, it creaked open to reveal an empty room. The second room housed a bed, which reminded him of a monastic cell. The third door opened to reveal a lamp with a tiny flame and a bed. The fourth door revealed a store room of sorts, the fifth door was another cell and lastly, the sixth door would not open. Trying to open it was impossible so he went back to ask the scribe if he could open the door, but he did not speak and looked at Sasha then turned back to his writing, so he went back to the corridor.

"There are no other rooms! It must be this one!"

Trying all manner of ways to enter the sixth room, he became frustrated, so slumped down to the floor and leant against a stone cold wall. Time passed until he went around all the doors again, this time however, he examined the fourth room by going inside. There were four boxes in here and a chest. Opening the first box revealed a nesting mouse who ran quickly away; the second box had only dusty straw within; the third had scrolls, all of which were blank and the fourth had nothing in. Lastly, there was the chest. Some effort was required to lift the heavy lid, which squeaked and moaned against being opened. It was if it didn't want to budge, until perseverance prevailed and it was open. Inside the chest was nothing. Sasha sighed and looked away from it, but as he did he noticed something odd, there was no bottom to the chest. Placing his hand in it, he reached to feel the base, but there was none, so he took the torch and threw it inside, to light up whatever was within. The torch had landed on a large stone step, the first on a spiral staircase that curved round to the right. Entering the chest, he descended the large stone steps that circled a deep grey pillar. Down and down he went until he came to the bottom. Looking upward, he saw the height of the room, which was larger than anticipated and its depth was vaster than expected and it was full of books. Volumes upon volumes were in here, all dusty and covered in dust-webs. A small trough surrounding the walls was bringing light, being filled with sweet oil which was lit, revealing the full extent of the chamber and amount of books within. There were so many and he didn't know where to start.

Was this a joke? Were all these books the wisdom of the world? Or was it in just one? Looking at the spines of the books, he read their titles, which informed him that it was a library of many types of literature. Yet he was looking for just the one, the Book of Books. Where was it? So he searched, scanning shelves and piles, brushing off dust from many a tome, tracing titles of volumes with his index fingers and plucking the odd text that he had heard of and yearned to read. But where was the book he wanted? It wasn't in the middle of the room, on a lectern adorned with sculpture of candles and priests that surrounded it. It wasn't on proud display anywhere, just merely a forgotten publication in a hidden library, miles away from anyone.

Pitcher's Bridle, The Secret Rose, Muir's Poetry, Ribak's Epigram, Zafih's Comparative Religions, Shahs of the Path, Glad's Index of Methodology, Tallis Major's Sonnets, The Petals of Knowing, Faure's Fables, Hengst Brabbige, Le Bib, The Modal Suite, Tower's Abridged Anecdotes, all rare books, were here gaining dust from years of unopened rest. Sasha wanted to read many of the books and flicked through pages of the books he plucked from the shelves. Turning a corner, he saw another person reading a volume, standing in front of the long set of shelves. The man appeared to be engrossed in the words pouring into his eyes, but he noticed Sasha looking at him.

"Ah, another seeker! And what, pray tell, are you looking for?"

"I am looking for the Book of Books. I'm led to believe it is here."

The librarian chuckled to himself and gazed at Sasha's appearance; a dusty, dirty brown tunic, dirt smudged face and short, wavy brown hair; sand covered, dirt stained feet and young, wrinkled hands, leathered from hard work.

"Have you travelled far?"

"From beyond the jungle and forest, I'm from the monastery on the hills."

"And you're after the Book of Books, eh?"

"Yes."

"Come with me..."

The librarian led Sasha around an aisle drawing him further into the heart of the library. Thousands, possibly a million, books lined the shelves giving off a slightly musty odour which wasn't unpleasant. They approached an area which had scores of scrolls and a large, wooden table nearby. The librarian made a gesture for Sasha to stop then he went to the bottom of a set of shelves and brought out a box. Placing it on the table, he blew sand and dust off then wiped it with a hand. Opening it up, he beckoned Sasha over.

This was it. The Book of Books, was here now, the book that contained the wisdom of the world.

"May I open it?"

"Yes, you may, yet only an enlightened mind can read the pages."

"Is it true that it contains the wisdom of all the world?"

"It has within the wisdom of the world, universe, everything!"

Sasha looked inside the box to see a large, thick book covered in cloth. Lifting it out, he unwrapped the book and set it down on the table. Its leather cover had no etching, letters, words or any sign of a title, yet this did not deter him from opening the cover. He closed his eyes for a moment then gazed at the frontispiece. 'The Book,' it said, with nothing underneath it. Turning the page, he saw large, old fashioned script that spelled, three words, one on each line; Perceive, Believe, Receive. Turning the page again, he seemed disappointed, so turned another page, then again and again. The dusty, yellowed sheets were blank. All of the rest of the pages had nothing on. Sasha frantically skipped through the pages, but saw no other text within.

"Like I said, only an enlightened mind can read the pages," said the librarian very quietly. "What you seek is within."

Sasha looked at the oldish man who moved his right hand in a motion to encourage the seeker to read again.

"Don't look for it, don't think about what you're looking at and you will see it."

Confused, Sasha thought about what was being said.

"If one looks for a tree, what will they see?"

"A tree," replied Sasha.

"So, if one looks for wisdom what will they see?'

"Wisdom."

He turned back to view the book and the pages were different. Slowly they revealed themselves to him and the blank pages came alive, for his mind had become open. Turning the blank pages, Sasha understood. Laughing, the librarian asked, "How did you manage to see it?"

"Well, like you said, what one looks for they find, so I looked for nothing and nothing was there, but it was full of something else."

"Not many can see it and so many walk away disappointed after looking on the book, so I like moments like these, when the veil lifts from someone's eyes. Tell me, what did you see?"

"I saw an old man and a child. He was about to write something down on a blank page, yet he didn't know exactly what he was going to write..."

THE GRANDFATHER'S TALE. *(For Jessica)*

"What are you writing, Grandad?"

The page was blank, as was the book. It was empty of words, yet full of thoughts, ponderings and musings which had not been written down as yet. Jessica watched her Grandad look up into his mind's eye, trying to capture it in words. Many of the idle thoughts from his youth were raw and untamed, needing the nurturing touch of age, to add flavour and make it palatable for the readers, who would eventually consume every morsel with their eyes. He was also mindful of those who would listen to his tale, like his granddaughter.

"Ooo, well, I'm writing a story."

"What's it about?"

"It's a bit about this and a lot about that."

"About what though?"

"It's about a little girl who asks what her Grandfather is writing in his book."

A playful smile formed on Jessica's lips. "What's the girl's name?"

"Ah! Now we need a name for her don't we... What's a good name for a girl?"

"Jessica – Jessica's a brilliant name!"

"It most certainly is! It's an excellent name in fact. Right then, so we have a name. Now what should the story be about?"

Jessica's bright eyes decided to look for inspiration and she decided to play the same game as Grandad.

"How about making it a bit about this and a lot about that?"

"Excellent idea! So, we begin writing our story, which is... Well, we're writing a story about writing a story at the moment, aren't we?"

"You're being silly, Grandad! Write a story for me!"

"Now that is truly a wonderful idea! So, I think I shall tell you about my life. I've had a long life and some of the things I have to say are, I believe, important. Would you like to hear my story?"

"Yes."

"Excellent! Right then, where shall I start? The beginning is always a superb place to start, isn't it?"

"Start at the end, Grandad."

"At the end? Good grief! What a funny start, to start with. Uhmm, I need to get my thinking cap on...."

The four year old wandered off and a moment later rummaging could be discerned from the clattering of plastic and cries from a baby doll. Walking back to the dining table, with an assured smile on her face, she held a pink baseball hat in her hand. A unicorn dancing in front of a rainbow graced the brow of the hat.

"There you go! I always use this cap when I'm thinking about things."

"My, my! That's a fantastic hat!"

The granddad adorned the article then placed his left hand under his chin and stroked his beard with the thumb. A few minutes passed until one of those elusive thoughts became snared in words. After some untangling, the first sentence was born.

"Now there are lots of things in this veritable universe besides catlets and doglings, like flutterflies and flutterbugs, dandehogs and ladylions, birdies and ballydogs, corpidons and snothogs, burpeesheeps and candybleets, chicklets and froglings, manbugs and moocows, meeces and hollerbats, horsenez and flitty-flights, mothlings and jitternits, helefumps and fishlets, and much more besides, all of whom have their tales to tell..."

So please tell me, dear reader, if you are able,
Who is the teller of these tales and fables?

INDEX.

Within this testament are tales; short tales, tall tales and those somewhere in-between, weaved with the wisdom diffused from petty crimes, witty rhymes, folklore and dreams, into a rhapsody of writing for the reader to relish. The characters tell tales that all ages will understand, about attitudes, behaviours and love for your neighbours; what's wrong and right and will give you insight into messages passed down since the inception of time, as well as those that are hidden between the lines.
This menagerie of morals is infused with light-hearted anecdotes, quips and quick witted wits, being easy on the eye and can be read in quiet, or aloud, with the most eloquent of lips.

And all I ask, dear reader, if you are able,
Is to tell me who is the overall teller of these tales and fables?

If you think you know who tells these tales,
Tell me, please dear reader, via email.

BeliefNexus@gmail.com

Also available from the same author:

Belief Nexus
The Time Traveler's Textbook
Belief Nexus 360* Journal
The Spiritual Pathfinder's Pocketbook

Printed in Great Britain
by Amazon

47786932R00168